The Treasure Key

The Crime Solving Cousins Mystery Series

The Feather Chase
The Treasure Key

The Treasure Key

A Crime-Solving Cousins Mystery

Shannon L. Brown

Sienna Bay Press

All rights reserved. For information about permission to reproduce selections from this book, write to:

Sienna Bay Press
PO Box 158582
Nashville, TN 37215

www.shannonlbrown.com

Copyright © 2016 Shannon L. Brown

The Treasure Key/Shannon L. Brown—1st ed.

ISBN: 978-0-9898438-5-0

Library of Congress Control Number: 2016903547

To my friend Katie,
Friends fill a special
place in our hearts.

Thank you for being
there for me
throughout the years.

1

Key to a Mystery

Jessica Ballow yawned and slouched into her chair. "We need *something* to do." Pine Hill had become every bit as boring as she'd imagined when her parents first told her she was going to spend the summer in this small town in the mountains. On top of that, she had to stay with her cousin Sophie, whom she hadn't seen since they were little. They got along well . . . now.

Sophie Sandoval fell backward onto the sofa. "Agreed. Maybe we should go into town."

"Why not? At least we won't just be sitting in your living room. We found our first mystery, *The Feather Chase,* right after I got here, so I barely had time to be bored." Jessica yawned. "Now I am."

"I doubt we'll find another mystery, even though I love mysteries—"

Jessica groaned. "I know. The next couple of months might be b-o-r-i-n-g." An endless summer of small-town life stretched in front of her.

"Pine Hill isn't boring."

A picture of lying on a sandy beach on Pine Lake with the sun overhead popped into Jessica's mind. "You're right. Let's get our swimsuits on."

This time Sophie slouched, her ponytail of brown hair smashing against the back of the sofa. "Again? We went to the beach yesterday. Wouldn't you like to go hiking on Cutoff Trail?"

The image in Jessica's mind switched to one of a trail climbing through a pine tree–lined path. With bugs. And wild animals. "*Like* isn't the word I'd use." When she paused, boredom began to sink in again. "I might not survive to my thirteenth birthday if I'm this bored. Let's do it."

Sophie instantly stood. "Really?"

"Pine Hill was way more exciting than home for a while. It's Tuesday, so most of a long week of nothing is in front of me. I'm ready to do something." Sometimes Jessica wished she could be with her parents, but they were on the other side of the world because of her father's job, and both she and her brother were spending the summer with relatives.

As Sophie ran into the room they were sharing, she said, "I think we'll both make it from twelve to thirteen, even if we are bored." She ran right back out with her backpack. "Let's go."

Jessica giggled as she followed Sophie to the door. "You aren't taking any chances that I'll change my mind, are you?"

"When the girl who loves shopping and is used to

living in big-city London, England, says she'll go on a hike, we're on our way out the door." She glanced at Jessica's feet and stopped. "Sneakers."

"I forgot." Jessica raced into their bedroom. After slipping off her pretty pink sandals, she put on her boring-but-useful white sneakers and hurried back. Standing at a mirror beside the front door, she checked her makeup and tucked her blonde hair behind her ears, saying, "Sophie, maybe we'll find another mystery on Cutoff Trail."

Sophie got a faraway look in her brown eyes and sighed. "Oh, that would be *amazing*." She opened the front door and stepped out.

With one foot in midair, she froze.

Jessica peered over her shoulder. "Is something wrong?"

Sophie stepped to the side and pointed down. Right in front of her sat a perfectly gift-wrapped package. The wrapping paper had tiny pine trees on a white background and was encircled with a forest green ribbon and bow.

"Is today a holiday I don't know about?"

"I don't think it's even Mom and Dad's anniversary or anything like that." Sophie picked up the box and shook it. "I can't feel anything moving around inside it." Stepping back into the house, she held the box close to her ear and shook it again. "I wonder if we should open it."

"What if it's supposed to be a surprise for your mom or dad?"

"I don't think someone would leave a package for one of them and not put their name on it."

Jessica said, "That made sense for a second. Then I thought, why would someone *ever* leave a package with no name on it? What if it's for you? Or even for me?"

"All good points." Sophie shifted from one foot to the other. "I'd like to see inside. But I really don't want to get in trouble."

Jessica reached for it. "I'll open it so it won't be your fault. I'm going home at the end of the summer, but you have to live here all the time."

Sophie grinned and handed her the box. "I like the way you think, Cousin."

Jessica carefully removed the wrapping paper and set it on the nearby dining room table. When she opened the lid, an old-looking, yellowed envelope with the word *Desk* handwritten on it lay inside. "Whoa."

"What is it?"

Jessica stared at the envelope. Had someone set a mystery on Sophie's doorstep? The odds were totally against finding another mystery so soon. Maybe even impossible. Laughing, Jessica stepped back from the box. "Hey, you set me up. You knew I was bored and you did this to cheer me up! Making the envelope appear old was a master touch."

Sophie leaned over and tried to see into the box. "Uh-uh. It wasn't me. Did you say there's an old envelope in there?"

"Yes." Jessica picked up the envelope. "And there's something inside." She rubbed the envelope between her fingers. "I think it's a key." A sense of excitement ran through her. "Could we have found another mystery?"

"On the doorstep? I agree with your first thought: someone's playing a joke on us." Sophie reached for the envelope. "Let's open it up." She pulled on the end to tear it.

"Wait! We may already be in trouble for opening the present—"

Sophie dropped the envelope as if it were on fire. "And get in much bigger trouble if we open this too." She stared at it. "I'll open it carefully, just in case it is a clue for a real mystery. Or mom or dad think it's important." She went into her mom's office, which was just off the living room. "Being careful doesn't mean I won't get in trouble, but maybe it will help."

When she returned with something that looked like a knife with fancy decorations, Jessica said, "You're kind of off the hook for opening the package, so maybe I should—"

"Good idea." Sophie handed the letter opener to Jessica. She carefully inserted it in the end of the envelope and made a clean cut before tilting it and dumping out a key that hit the table with a clunk.

They both stared at it.

Sophie said, "I want to get excited about all of this. But I keep feeling like I should look over my shoulder for someone who's making a video of us opening their package. I don't know if it's a pretend mystery, or if another real mystery has landed at our feet."

"Cousin, you're the mystery expert. If you don't know, we're in trouble."

Sophie stood straighter. "You're right. I've read so many mystery books and watched so many mystery movies that I am an expert." She picked up the box. "Let's start with crime-solving basics and examine the clues."

Jessica smoothed out the wrapping paper. "Basic Christmas paper. Except that I'd put a red bow on it to make it more Christmassy. Anything interesting with the box?"

Sophie turned it from side to side, then set it back down. "No." She snapped her fingers. "I wonder . . ." Quickly grabbing the paper, she flipped it over. Frowning, she said, "Blank."

Jessica grinned. "Did you think there'd be a message written on the back?"

Sophie sheepishly nodded. "It could happen."

"Maybe it's in invisible ink."

"Maybe," Sophie slowly said.

Jessica could tell Sophie was intrigued by the idea for a second. Then she set it down.

"Nah. I think it's just wrapping paper. We could take it by the sheriff's office. We haven't visited Sheriff Valeska in a couple of weeks."

"Yes. She told you to come back"—Jessica changed her voice to sound like the sheriff—"if and when you found another mystery."

"It was fun working with her last time. I hope we get to do it again."

"Speaking of solving mysteries"—Jessica leaned over the table—"this paper seems familiar."

"I don't remember seeing it before, but it looks like a thousand other Christmas wrapping papers."

"That's it!" Jessica picked up the gift wrap. "Remember all that time I spent cleaning out the back room of your mother's antique shop, Great Finds?"

"Sure. While you cleaned out the back room, I dusted and did other stuff."

"I think this was old wrapping paper your mom had there. I remember her saying that she thought the pine trees would be right for a store in Pine Hill, but everyone said it looked like Christmas paper so she stopped using it."

"You mean Mom might have set us up?" Sophie glared at the box. "I wonder if she thought this would be funny."

Jessica shook her head. "I've been here long enough to know that doesn't sound like my Aunt April. She doesn't seem like the sneaky type."

"I've been so sad since we solved the last mystery that she might be trying to help." Sophie walked through the living room and peered down the hall. "The door to Dad's office is closed, so we'd better not bother him. I think Mom said something about him being extra busy right now with his accounting business."

She dropped the key back in the envelope and

handed it to Jessica. "Here. I don't need my backpack just to go to town, and this will get less rumpled in your purse than it will in my back pocket." She headed for the door. "Let's go talk to Mom." Sophie stopped halfway down the steps. "Are you okay with taking the shortcut through the woods, or should we walk along the road?"

"Shortcut. The sheriff arrested the bad guys that chased us when we were trying to solve our last mystery, so we're safe walking through the woods again."

As they walked down the path, Jessica stepped on a branch, and it made a loud cracking sound. She wiped her brow with her hand. "Whew. I'm so glad I don't need to worry about hearing someone else making that sound when we're supposed to be *alone* in the woods."

"I know. Part of me is happy that life is quiet again."

At the edge of Pine Hill, Sophie yelled, "Race you!" and took off.

Jessica ran after her. When she could see Main Street, Sophie was leaning against the brick front of Simpson's Shoes.

"You're getting slow, Jessica. A twelve-year-old should have more energy."

Jessica leaned over, panting. "It's only been a couple of weeks since I had to be fast on my feet. We need to do something so I don't get out of shape."

"Since we aren't going hiking today, Cutoff Trail tomorrow?" Sophie looked so excited that Jessica didn't have the heart to tell her no.

"Sure. We'll find out what's going on with the box and envelope today. Tomorrow we go hiking."

They walked the short distance to Great Finds. When they pushed the glass door to the shop open, a bell rang and a voice called from the back room, "Welcome to Great Finds. I'll be right with you."

Jessica pulled the envelope out of her purse and tipped the key into Sophie's hand.

Sophie peered around the shop, probably checking to be sure they were alone. When Mrs. Sandoval stepped into the shop itself, Sophie held up the key. "Mom, was this a joke?"

Mrs. Sandoval walked toward them, smiling. "I'm glad you figured out the wrapping-paper clue. I hoped you would."

"You played a joke on us? Mom!"

"There *is* a real mystery." She pointed to the front of the shop.

Sophie raised one eyebrow. "It's a big piece of furniture. There aren't any drawers on the front, and something curved is over the top of it, but I kind of think it's a desk. Right?"

"A special desk, a cylinder desk. A curved piece of wood rolls over the top. The owner could leave their work on the desktop, roll the top down to hide it and lock up when they finished for the day."

"It's still just a desk."

The three walked together to where the desk sat. Jessica smoothed her hand over the curved cover. "The whole desk is beautiful." She leaned to see the side. "I love the flower design on it." Old furniture, dishes, lamps, even jewelry, filled Great Finds. But this desk seemed as though it had been around longer than most of the things her aunt had for sale. "Is it old?" she asked.

"Oh, yes. It was made in the 1700s." Mrs. Sandoval stared at the desk in a way Jessica could only describe as lovingly. She sighed and said, "It's exquisite."

"Let's see if the key fits." Sophie tried to insert it in the lock on the front of the cylinder. "The key is too big."

"I know." Mrs. Sandoval reached over to the cashier stand and picked up another key. "When it arrived, this key was in that keyhole. The envelope with your key was tucked into a cubbyhole, a storage space inside the desk." She smiled widely. "I did seal the envelope, though, to add an air of mystery."

Sophie flipped the key in her hand, and Jessica grabbed it in midair, saying, "Maybe it's to another desk."

"I don't know what desk that would be. This is the only desk the man was known to have owned, at least in his later years." Mrs. Sandoval walked over and flipped the sign on the door to Closed. "I have to go to a meeting, so I'm going to close for a while."

Sophie stood proudly. "We could watch the shop for you, Mom."

Jessica pictured the problems that could come up. Sometimes Sophie had a way of finding trouble.

Mrs. Sandoval raised one eyebrow.

"Okay, so maybe I wasn't good at doing that once. But I can!"

Mrs. Sandoval shook her head. "I'm not ready to try that again. I rarely close during the day, but this meeting is important." She stepped out the door, and the girls followed her outside.

As she was locking the door, she said, "The desk belonged to Harold Laurence."

Sophie shrugged. "Never heard of him."

"Yes, you have. You just don't remember the name. He owned that big old house on the hill overlooking Pine Lake. He died a few years ago at 102 years old."

Jessica furrowed her brow. "If he died years ago, how did you get his desk now?"

"That's an interesting story, Jessica. Mr. Laurence said in his will that it had to stay in Pine Hill. I knew it was sitting in that big empty house all these years, so I asked about it."

Sophie said, "But you have customers from lots of places. One might buy it and take it away from here."

"No. I worked with the estate's lawyers, and whoever buys it has to agree to keep it in Pine Hill. It's a beauty with a story attached to it, so I thought it would be good to have it in my shop, even if it didn't sell right away because of its high price."

As the three walked away from the shop front, she added, "The rumor of a lost treasure makes anything from Mr. Laurence more interesting."

2

Hidden Clues

They hadn't made it five steps before Sophie spun around and started to head back toward the door to Great Finds. Before she could get out of reach, her mother grabbed her sleeve. "Sophie, where are you going?"

"I need to see the desk again. You didn't tell us about a treasure." Sophie peered over her shoulder at her mother, who hadn't moved an inch back toward her business.

"Soph, the key didn't fit anything on the desk. I thought I'd spice up your day, but I don't have time for this."

"Please, Mom. I have to see if there's something hidden in the desk. You said the envelope was inside a cubbyhole. Maybe one of the cubbyholes has a lock and we missed it, or something else inside the desk does." Sophie pleaded with her eyes. "Maybe there's a *treasure* inside."

Mrs. Sandoval slumped. Looking at her watch, she

said, "Twenty minutes. The meeting's across town, and I was going to walk, but I'll drive instead." Putting the key in the front door lock, she added, "You'll have to come back later if you aren't successful in that amount of time."

Sophie ran over to the desk, lay down on the floor, and scooted under the front part of the desk where the chair would go.

Jessica's green eyes stared down at her. "Uh, Sophie, what are you doing?"

Sophie lifted her head up. "In detective shows there's often something taped underneath furniture. There aren't any drawers, but I thought maybe . . ." There was silence for a moment as Sophie rooted around under the desk.

Jessica asked, "Find anything?"

Sophie scooted back out. "Nope. Jessica, check the outside of the desk, and I'll see if there's anything else in the cubbyholes and the rest of the inside."

Mrs. Sandoval tapped her watch. "You have seventeen minutes."

Jessica crouched in front of the desk. "What are we looking for?"

"Anything that doesn't seem right."

A moment later, the girls heard, "Sixteen minutes."

"I can't work like this, Mom!"

Mrs. Sandoval started for the back room. "I'm going into the back to pack up something I need to ship later."

"Good idea, Mom."

When Mrs. Sandoval stepped into the back room, Sophie whispered, "I think I can focus on this now that she isn't telling me the time every minute."

Jessica stared at the desk. "It doesn't seem right to me that the desk doesn't have drawers."

Sophie leaned back to see the front. "True. There's a big space on the left side where drawers would usually be."

Jessica rubbed her hand over the front of the desk. Then she leaned in and looked underneath in the place where the chair would fit and ran her hand over the sides there. When Jessica continued to the left and to the underside of the area too low to the floor to slide under, she jumped in surprise. "Sophie, there's a bump here."

Sophie crouched beside her. "It's old. Is it just a broken piece?"

"This is odd," Jessica said. "I wonder . . ." She pushed on the spot, and the front of the left side of the desk popped out.

"Oh no! Mom is not going to be happy. I hope it can be fixed." Sophie leaned down and checked under the piece, moving it slightly up and down. As she lifted it, a large drawer became visible. "It's a door." When she'd raised the door all the way, she gently pushed it out of the way into what appeared to be a slot made for it.

The two of them silently stared at the hidden compartment for a few seconds before Sophie said, "Wow."

Jessica said, "Wow is right, Sophie."

Sophie pointed. "There's a keyhole."

Jessica pulled the key from the envelope out of her purse and handed it to Sophie.

"I'd better be very careful. Mom said this was old *and* valuable."

Jessica leaned over Sophie as she tried the key.

"Doesn't fit. Let's try the small one that fit the top."

Sophie felt her heart speed up as the key slid into the lock. "This is it!" She turned it to the right, and the whole drawer popped forward, pushing her to the floor. As she scrambled to her feet, Jessica peered inside.

Standing up, Sophie asked, "What's inside? Is there a treasure map?"

Jessica answered. "Not a thing."

"Nothing? A key opens a hidden drawer and there isn't anything in that drawer?"

"I don't have any answers, Soph. Maybe Mr. Laurence liked the desk, but didn't keep anything in it."

Sophie squatted in front of the drawer. "I'm not giving up yet. Let's check for something taped to the top."

Jessica shrugged. "Why not?"

Sophie felt around inside the drawer area. "The top is clear. Maybe we should pull the drawer out and check behind it."

"That sounds like something you should ask your mom."

"Probably. Mom!"

Mrs. Sandoval hurried over. "Is something wrong?"

"No, Mom." Sophie pointed at the desk.

Kneeling in front of it, Mrs. Sandoval said, "This is exciting."

"Mom, can we pull the drawer out to see if something's hidden behind it?"

"I don't see why not," her mom answered, "provided that we aren't damaging it in any way. But let me do it." She bent over and gently pulled the drawer forward. "It stopped."

Sophie leaned closer. "It won't come out? Are you sure? All of the drawers in our furniture at home come out."

Mrs. Sandoval turned, her eyes suspicious. "How do you know that?"

Sophie felt her cheeks turn pink. "I checked to make sure nothing was hidden behind them. It was in the book I was reading."

Mrs. Sandoval chuckled. "I will say that you're right, Sophie. Drawers can usually be removed."

Sophie crouched beside her. "Jessica found a button for the cover. Maybe there's another one that makes the drawer removable." She felt around inside the drawer. "Hey, here in the back there's a piece that seems loose."

"Careful. If the wood is cracked or broken, don't make it worse."

"It has smooth edges, so it doesn't feel like a broken piece." Sophie stood and moved to the left of the desk, bending over to reach inside. "This time, I'm not going to stand in front when I push it. Let's see what happens."

When she pushed on the wood, the drawer jumped forward and swung to the left, shoving her backward. She landed on the floor—again.

Jessica laughed. "You may be onto something. I know by watching you what I shouldn't do."

"Ha-ha."

Sophie crawled around the corner and looked into the open space. "There are hidden drawers behind the hidden drawer! Three of them!" She reached for the top drawer handle. "Maybe there's treasure inside."

Jessica said, "A tiny treasure. Two of those drawers aren't more than an inch deep."

"Diamonds are tiny," Sophie said.

Sophie pulled the three drawers open one by one. "Nothing . . . Nothing."

When she opened the third drawer, the largest one, she froze.

"Is there something in it?" Jessica asked as she and Sophie's mom leaned in closer.

"It's a piece of paper. Maybe it has a treasure map on it." Sophie reached into the third drawer and pulled it out, then said, "It's just a photo of a house with 'Hilltop' written on it." She handed it to her mom.

Mrs. Sandoval scrunched up her face as she studied the picture. "That's the Laurence house. Both the house and grounds have changed a lot since this was taken, and not for the better." She pointed at the faded photo. "This building has the same tow

er on each corner. It's definitely his house."

Jessica peered into the drawer. "Anything else in there?" She reached into the drawer. "Empty."

Mrs. Sandoval stood. "I have to run now. Please come back this afternoon and dust for me. Right now, why don't you get some lunch at Donadio's Deli?" She reached into her purse, checking her watch at the same time. Handing Sophie some money, she added, "I'll be back in an hour. Two at the most." Then she turned and headed for the door.

Jessica put the key back in the envelope and slid it into her purse.

Waving the girls over, Mrs. Sandoval opened the door. "I can just make my meeting." She hurried them outside, locked up, and rushed down the sidewalk to her car, parked nearby on the street.

As she unlocked her car door, she looked back at them and said, "Maybe go see Nezzy." Before they could answer, she climbed into the car, started it, and drove away, waving as she passed them.

Sophie and Jessica stared at each other. "Did you understand what Mom said?"

"I heard the words but don't understand. What's a *Nezzy*? There's a Loch Ness monster in a lake in Scotland, and they call it Nessie. We went to the lake for a weekend once, but didn't see the monster. I doubt she meant that. Anyway, it's mystery break time! Maybe we can go shopping after lunch."

Sophie swallowed hard. If they had to decide

between doing something outdoors, like hiking or fishing, or shopping, Sophie would *always* pick the outdoors. She said, "Let's go with food first. I definitely can't think about shopping when I'm hungry."

Jessica laughed. "I can always think about shopping. Maybe your mother will take us sometime."

Sophie hoped her face didn't give away how much she *didn't* want that to happen anytime soon. "Let's go to lunch at the deli. Tony's mother is usually there. Maybe she'll know what 'Nezzy' means."

"I'm always happy to eat at the deli. They make good food."

"They do. But you might also like to see Tony there today."

Jessica stared at the ground. "He's a friend of yours, too."

"Yes. But he's never given me a hot fudge sundae, and he did give you one."

"You're right." When Jessica looked up, Sophie grinned.

3

What's a Nezzy?

A smiling, older man brushed by the girls as they stepped through the door into Donadio's Deli. Sophie knew she'd seen him before but couldn't remember who he was.

She and Jessica walked up to the counter. Jessica got a silly grin on her face as Tony, the owner's dark-haired son, took their order. Once they'd ordered their sandwiches, they went to find a table.

As they sat and waited for their food, Sophie tapped her fingers on the table. She still couldn't remember who that man was, and it was starting to bug her. When Tony brought their lunches, she asked him.

"He's Mr. Jenkins, and he must be the nicest man in town. He took good care of Mr. Laurence as his butler when he was alive, and lives in the house now as the caretaker. He comes here almost every day and talks about what a great man Mr. Laurence was. He says he does that to keep his memory alive."

"I think Mom and Dad had him over for dinner once when I was young. Mom said something about a 'Nezzy' today. Would you ask your mom if she knows what a Nezzy is?"

Tony laughed as he leaned against the table. "I can answer that. Nezzy isn't a what. It's a who." He clearly liked knowing something she didn't.

"Okay. *Who* is Nezzy?"

"Nezzy Grant. You know Mrs. Grant."

"Oh. Sure, I do." Sophie smacked her forehead with her hand. Turning to Jessica, she said, "Nezzy is old lady Grant, and she must be a hundred years old."

Tony stood. "She's ninety-nine. I know because she loves our chicken salad sandwiches, and that's what she wanted for her ninety-ninth birthday lunch."

Sophie popped a chip in her mouth as Tony headed back to the counter. "We don't have time to visit Nezzy and go to Hilltop today before we need to go back to Great Finds to help Mom."

Jessica took a sip of her lemonade. "I've never been to Hilltop, and it was Mr. Laurence's house. I say we go there."

Lowering her voice and glancing around to make sure no one could hear her, Sophie said, "Maybe holding up the photo and looking at the house at the same time will show us something important." She ate another chip, then bit into her sandwich.

"Kind of like the game where you have to see what's different between the two pictures." Jessica spread some extra mustard on her turkey sandwich.

"Yes."

"I've always liked that game."

Just then Jessica's phone made a frog's *ribbit-ribbit* sound, and Sophie knew a message had come in from Jessica's brother.

Her cousin pulled out her phone. "I guess Dona-dio's Deli is one of the few places in Pine Hill where cell phone reception is good. I just wish my phone worked at your house."

"Cell phones and Pine Hill definitely aren't good together. The mountains block the signal most of the time, but at least the mountains are pretty."

Jessica turned her phone so Sophie could see it. "Frog Boy sent a photo of himself with a giant fish he caught off Uncle Bill's fishing boat."

"Are you sure your brother doesn't mind being called Frog Boy?"

"He didn't mind when he was really little," Jessica answered, then frowned. "I might have to start calling him Jake now that he's almost ten."

After tucking her phone away, she asked, "Do you know where Hilltop is?"

"Everyone in Pine Hill knows that house," Sophie said. "I just didn't recognize it in the photo. Mom took me there a couple of years ago for a party the city had for people who helped out with Hilltop. I remember that it's kind of creepy, even driving in."

"We need to ask the owners if we can see it."

"The city owns it, so I guess it would be like going to a park. I don't think we can go inside without asking

Mom or Dad. There might be an awesome clue to the treasure on the outside though."

"Right," Jessica said. "It's been sitting outside the house, and no one else noticed it. Not in close to a hundred years."

"It could happen."

"Sure." Jessica took another bite of her sandwich. After she'd swallowed, she said, "We don't know if there really is a treasure. Your mom said there was a 'rumor' of lost treasure. That means it may or may not be true."

Sophie shoved the last bite—maybe two bites—of her sandwich into her mouth. When she'd swallowed, with the help of her drink, she stood. "Some people believe it. I plan to be one of those." Sophie could picture the looks on everyone's faces when she found the treasure. She took a step toward the door. "Are you coming?"

Jessica ate the last bite of her sandwich, then said, "Let's go."

"Another mystery." Sophie waved her on.

Jessica groaned but joined her. "Here we go again."

"Admit it. You're a little less bored now. You're happier."

"I am happier." She paused. "As long as there aren't any bad guys, especially any bad guys *chasing us*."

4

Mysterious Mansion

Going out of the deli, Jessica followed Sophie as she turned right and headed up the street. Sophie pointed beyond Pine Lake and said, "Hilltop's over there. I think Mr. Laurence's house used to have a great view of the lake, but trees and bushes grew up in front of it. Now you can barely see it even when you're in a boat."

Once they'd walked past the lake and beyond the downtown area, Sophie turned left onto a narrow, gravel driveway filled with potholes and overhung by trees. Even though it was a sunny day, it was cooler and felt like dusk with all the shadows under the trees.

"Spooky," Jessica said.

"I told you it had a haunted-house thing going on. And you haven't even seen the house yet."

Breathing hard, Jessica stopped. "I also see why it's called Hilltop. We're definitely going uphill."

"I know," Sophie answered, also stopping. "Mr. Laurence must have seen everything around here from his windows, sitting above the town, the lake, everything—when you could still see through the trees and brush, that is."

They continued up the sloping drive and soon came around a curve, where a massive house sat in front of them. Jessica pulled out the photo and held it up. "It's no wonder your mother didn't recognize the house in the photo at first. It was a beautiful mansion, and now it looks like it might fall down any minute!"

"It has some holes in the roof—"

"*Big* holes in the roof."

"But the city says it's safe." Sophie walked over to the side of the house and pushed on it. "See, the walls are still standing."

"This is brick, so people here must have liked bricks for a long time. I'm still surprised at all of the brick buildings in this town." Jessica stared at a hole in the corner of the roof that overhung them. "Why is a mansion like this in such bad shape? The owner must have been rich to have built this."

"I don't think he had much money when he got old."

Jessica started to step forward, then paused. "Didn't Tony say Mr. Jenkins was the butler? Poor people don't have butlers."

"True. I don't know the story, but Mom will. Anyway, Mr. Laurence didn't have kids, so he left the house to the city in his will. I don't know why it's such a mess."

"I think it would be very expensive to repair. It isn't just the holes in the roof. They must have let in a lot of rain—and other things—over the years." Jessica pointed at the roof. "There's a bird's nest at the edge of that hole. Maybe the city doesn't have enough money sitting around to fix everything."

Sophie surveyed the area. "You're probably right. It would cost thousands of dollars to fix all of this."

"Thousands and thousands."

"Let's walk around the house and look for clues."

"I ask again: what would give us a clue to a treasure's hiding place? If there is a treasure."

Sophie started to speak, but Jessica held up her hand to stop. "We don't even know if the photo was an actual clue to the treasure."

"Of course it's a clue. Remember that the last time I told you we'd found a mystery, we really had."

"That's true," Jessica said. "But that doesn't mean you're right again. Maybe Mr. Laurence was just sentimental. He likes holding on to things with memories, so he kept an old photo."

"Jessica, the man had a treasure, and we found the photo hidden in a secret area of his desk."

"People *believe* that he had a treasure. He might have just liked this photo and wanted to keep it safe."

"Stop being so negative. Clues are often in unexpected places."

"At least we have something to do." Jessica waved Sophie forward.

Sophie had that *I'm on the trail of a mystery* look. "I just know we'll find something exciting."

As they continued around the house, Jessica said,

"It must have been pretty here." She pointed to their left. "I think there used to be a flower garden with a rock wall, like we have in England. Now there's just a pile of rocks."

As they neared the corner of the house, Jessica pointed to the edge of the roof. "There's another giant hole." She took steps backward until she could see more of the roof.

Sophie pointed at the hole. "A squirrel darted inside it." Laughing, she started to turn toward Jessica.

Jessica watched what happened next as if in slow motion. Someone raced around the corner of the house, swinging his hands around in the air, and slammed sideways into Sophie. As she started to fall, Jessica raced toward her and prayed she'd get to her before she hit the rocks.

A man and woman followed the blur around the corner, and the man grabbed Sophie's arm, stopping her fall.

"Are you okay, Sophie?" Jessica asked when she got to her side.

Sophie leaned against the house. When she reached up, her hand was shaking. "I thought I was going to land face-first in those rocks."

Jessica turned and saw a girl a few years older than them standing beside the man and woman now. The woman asked Sophie, "Are you injured?"

"No. I'm fine." Sophie straightened and turned toward the man. It didn't take her long to recover. "Thank you for catching me."

The man spoke. "We're the Coopers. These are our kids, Madeline and Cody."

"Cody?" Jessica hadn't noticed a boy about their age. Then she realized he'd been the blur.

Sophie glared at Cody. "You ran into me."

His face turned bright red. "I had hornets circling around me. I was trying to get away from them. I'm sorry you almost got hurt."

Sophie rolled her eyes and muttered, "City boy," just loud enough for Jessica to hear. She then thanked the boy's parents and moved quickly around the corner of the house, with Jessica right behind her.

"It's too bad he's a jerk," Sophie said. "He's cute."

Jessica stopped in her tracks. "What did you say?"

"Huh? I said he's a jerk."

"No. After that."

Sophie blushed. "Well, he *is* cute."

"Yes, he is. But I didn't think you'd notice. You hadn't paid any attention to Tony."

Sophie laughed. "Tony and I played together when we were babies. He's like a brother. Ick."

"Well, I think Cody *tried* to be nice and apologize to you."

Sophie looked around and tapped her foot. "He did, didn't he?"

Jessica nodded.

Whirling around in the other direction, Sophie said, "I could have been a little bit nicer to him."

"A little bit?"

Sophie's face turned a darker shade of red. "Maybe

a lot. But it hurt when he slammed into me." Pointing to the house, she said, "Let's get to work. Pull out the photo of Hilltop and hold it up."

Jessica did, and they both glanced from the photo to the house and back again. "One difference is that the photo is of a house with a whole roof, and this one only has part of a roof."

Sophie shrugged. "My first idea might not work. The house is in worse shape than I remembered. We'd better do some actual detective work. Walk around the house and see if anything stands out. See if there are any clues."

Sophie turned one direction, and Jessica the other, studying the house as they went. When they finally met on the other side, Jessica asked, "Did you see anything helpful?"

"Uh, no." She stared up at the house. "I keep hoping something will stand out."

"I don't see any clues."

Sophie frowned. "Me neither."

Jessica would rather get a milkshake at the resort or do something else fun instead of working on the maybe-mystery, but Sophie looked so sad that she said, "Tomorrow morning we can go meet Nezzy Grant. Maybe she can give you—or rather, us—some help."

Sophie perked up. "Great idea. We go to the next place for clues."

5

No Time to Lose

Two hours had passed by the time Sophie and Jessica hurried back into Great Finds. Mrs. Sandoval was helping a customer, so the two girls quietly stepped to the other side of the shop to wait.

Sophie watched as Jessica spun slowly in a circle. "Uh, Sophie, what's different about this picture?"

"Huh. Are you saying—" Sophie immediately looked at the place where the desk had sat earlier. She walked through the shop and came back to Jessica. "It's gone! Mom must have sold it."

Sophie paced back and forth by the front windows, impatiently watching her mother taking her time with her customer. Finally, she said quietly to Jessica, "Maybe the person who bought it will let us check it out if we need to."

Jessica stared at Sophie.

"Well, they might," Sophie said hopefully.

It seemed to take forever for her mom to finish helping the customer and ring up the purchase. As soon as the woman opened the door to leave, Sophie and Jessica hurried toward the cash register. When they were halfway across the room, Sophie blurted out, "Mom, who bought the desk?"

Mrs. Sandoval smiled. "Someone close to you. Don't worry."

When Sophie started to speak, Mrs. Sandoval said, "Just a minute. I have to write this down before I forget it." She made a note on a pad, then looked up. "Sorry for keeping you in suspense. Ever since we discovered the hidden drawers, I've thought about that desk. I finally decided that I didn't want to let it go. At least not yet. So I had it taken to our house, and it's in my office." She pointed across the room. "There's my old desk."

A couple entered the shop just then, and she went over to help them.

Sophie leaned against the counter, feeling dazed. "It's at our house," she whispered.

"Even I was a little nervous," Jessica said. "I don't want to lose the one place where we've found a clue—if it is a clue, which we aren't sure about." She shook her head as though she needed to clear it. "I didn't want it to be gone forever—just in case."

The customers left after browsing, and Mrs. Sandoval came back and dropped into a chair. "Other than the fun with the desk, my morning didn't turn out as I'd hoped."

"What happened?" Sophie asked.

"We need to protect treasures from the past. I tried

to explain that, but I lost the battle. The city council voted to tear down Hilltop. It will be taken to the ground in a month."

Jessica gulped. "That fast?" The clock was ticking on solving this mystery.

"It costs them every month to keep it. I had hoped that the town would find the money to restore the house and turn it into a convention center or art center, something that could be used by a lot of people. Instead, the land, all thirty acres of it, will be a park." She stood. "I guess that will have to be okay."

Sophie and Jessica followed her to the back room, where she retrieved a couple of dust rags. She started to hand them to the girls, then snatched them back before they could take them. "Let's do this another day," she said, as she laid the rags down where she'd found them, before heading back onto the sales floor.

Sophie watched her mother walk to the front of her shop and stare out the window. "I've never seen Mom like this. I sure hope we can find the treasure in time to save the house."

"Me too! It could be a beautiful house again."

Walking home, Sophie said, "Remind me when we get home to put the key in my secret hiding place."

"That is so cool! How many people find a hidden metal box under a loose floorboard in their closet?"

"We have to remember to put everything we find for the mystery into the box."

"If everything fits."

"Last time our clues were pretty small."

The phone was ringing when they stepped in the door, but it stopped ringing before Sophie could answer it.

"Is that you, Sophie and Jessica?" Lucas Sandoval called.

They both answered, "Yes."

"Jessica, your mom and dad are on the phone. You can use the phone in my office."

Jessica ran out of the room, wearing a huge smile. When she came back a short time later, she was grinning from ear to ear.

"Mom says it's very expensive to call from where they are, but she knows cell phones and texting aren't reliable here." Jessica sat down. "It feels so good to talk to them. I'm used to having Mom around all the time, so this summer has been strange."

"Do you think both your mom and dad will come back to London this fall?" asked Sophie.

Jessica gave a dreamy sigh. "That would be so nice. Sometimes I wish Dad had a normal job that didn't take him all over the world."

After dinner, the girls were sitting on the couch when Sophie said, "We went to see Hilltop today, Mom."

Mrs. Sandoval set down the newspaper she'd been reading. "Find any treasure?"

Mr. Sandoval groaned. "Don't tell me you girls are searching for the Laurence treasure now."

"Sure, Uncle Lucas. Do you want to see the photo we found in Mr. Laurence's desk today?"

"Why not?"

Sophie ran to her room to get the photo from its hiding place. When she returned, she gave it to her father.

Once he'd checked it out, he handed the photo back to Sophie. "You found an old photo in an old desk. That isn't surprising."

"It's a clue," Sophie said with confidence. "Now we need to see if there are more clues inside Hilltop."

Mrs. Sandoval said, "I don't want you inside the house without one of us. Mr. Jenkins lives there. It's his home, even if it does belong to the city."

"Can you or Dad come with us tomorrow?" Sophie asked.

"I wish I could, Soph, but I was closed quite a while today and can't do that again tomorrow. And I know your dad's been working on a special project that needs to be completed as soon as possible. Just stay outside the house."

Sophie sighed. "Okay." As she picked up the remote so she could put on a mystery movie, she muttered, "We have to find a way to get inside."

6

Any Body Here?

Sophie eyed Jessica warily from her bed the next morning, watching her cousin stretch and yawn.

"Don't worry," Jessica said. "I didn't wake up grumpy like I do sometimes."

Sophie raised one eyebrow, but didn't say a word.

"It could be more than *sometimes*."

Sophie nodded slowly, but still didn't say anything.

"When I wake up excited about the day ahead, it pushes all of my grumpiness away."

Jessica threw back the covers and got out of bed.

Sophie stared at her. "You *seem* okay."

"I think I'll get in the shower first thing, just to make sure. That always wakes me up completely. I wouldn't want to promise what I can't deliver."

Sophie slipped into her robe and tied the belt. "I'll have a breakfast surprise for you when you get up."

As Sophie cooked, a plan started and grew in her mind. She *thought* she could talk Jessica into it.

When Jessica walked into the kitchen, she sniffed

appreciatively. "Yum. I wondered what you'd make since I've only seen you cook dinner, and a stir-fry sounds rather unpleasant at 9:00 a.m."

"French toast." Sophie set a plate with two slices of French toast and some strawberries on the table, then sprinkled powdered sugar on top.

Jessica sat down and took a bite. "This is sooo good."

Sophie sat next to her. "I can show you how to make it. You could surprise your mom and brother."

Jessica put another bite into her mouth. "Dad would love this when he gets to come home from his job."

Sophie took a shower after breakfast. She thought that by the time she'd dried her hair and dressed, Jessica would be done with her hair and makeup and they could leave. She was wrong.

Sophie perched on the end of her bed and watched her cousin put on blush and lip gloss, things she'd only recently learned the names for. If someone had a question about how to put up a tent, she could help. Jessica didn't have a clue. She was girly all the time.

A glimmer from Jessica's teeth caught Sophie's eye. "Do braces hurt?" she asked.

Jessica stopped with an earring halfway to her ear and stared in the mirror. "Sometimes. But generally not. I'll be super glad when they're removed next year."

"I don't usually notice they're there."

After putting in the earring, Jessica said, "That's what Mom tells me." She inserted the other earring and added, almost in a whisper, "I wish she was here," reminding Sophie of how good it was to always have both her mom and dad with her.

Standing tall, Jessica turned her head from side to side in the mirror, Sophie figured to make sure she'd done a good job. Nodding once, she turned to face Sophie. "I'm ready to go."

Halfway through the living room on their way out of the house, the phone rang, and Sophie answered. Right after she'd said, "Hello," their plans for the morning were thrown out the window. Her heart sank as her mom talked.

"But we want to visit Nezzy today."

Her mother told her that they could visit Nezzy later, to remember that the old woman was eccentric and to be respectful—but first, they had a job to do.

After hanging up, Sophie sat down on the couch. "That was Mom."

"I could tell. We have a new project at her shop, don't we?"

"No." She gestured around the room. "Vacuuming, dusting, picking up."

Jessica plopped down next to Sophie. "Maybe it won't take too long."

"I think we can get out of here in about an hour. Let's make some cheese sandwiches for lunch and take them with us. We can head over to Nezzy's this afternoon, then get a ride home with Mom."

"Sounds good. Well, I shouldn't say that cleaning sounds *good*."

"Never." Sophie stood and held out her hand to help Jessica up. "Let's get this done. Then we can have our lunches at a picnic table in a park before we go see Nezzy. I know the perfect place."

"Have I been there before?"

"No. It's Dogwood Park, on the other side of town. I have an idea, and this will be good. By the way, Miss Smarty Pants, what's 'eccentric'?"

"Unusual. Maybe a little odd."

"That's how Mom described Nezzy. I can handle odd."

"I'm used to odd, being around you all the time." Jessica grinned and ducked.

"*Funny.*" Sophie tapped her cousin on the shoulder with her fist.

They ate at a wooden picnic table in a park that had tall pine trees. It might be a pretty place to sit and admire—if Sophie hadn't fidgeted like she was nervous about something. When they'd finished their lunches, Jessica picked up their trash and said, "You're acting like something's wrong. What's going on?"

"Since we haven't been able to get inside Hilltop, there's only one other place tied to Mr. Laurence that I know of where we haven't checked for clues."

Jessica furrowed her brow. "Where?"

"You aren't going to like it." Sophie winced. "*I* don't really like it."

"You're making me nervous. Just say it."

"It's a place where we won't see many people."

Jessica glared. "Another hike?"

"The cemetery."

Jessica looked heavenward. "Uh-uh. No way. I'm not going there." She stared at Sophie for a minute before speaking again. "I guess I should calm down enough to ask—why?"

"In the book I'm reading—"

"Oh, now I see. They found a clue inscribed on a tombstone?"

"On the cemetery's entrance sign. We've seen stranger things than that."

Jessica nodded once. "You're right about that. Okay."

Sophie took a step backward. "You'll go?"

"Other than being irrationally afraid—terrified, actually—that something creepy, like a body moaning in a grave, will happen there, I can't find any *good* reasons to say no."

"I think we're safe. It's just a few blocks from here."

"Now it all makes sense, Sophie. We passed two other parks on the way here, not to mention the picnic area by the beach."

"I thought that already being near the cemetery when I mentioned it would mean I could talk you into it more easily, and we would have a short walk to get there once you said yes."

"You mean *I* wouldn't have time to back out."

Sophie just grinned.

Neither girl said anything as they walked the five or six blocks to the cemetery at the edge of town. When they could see it ahead, Jessica glanced around. They were in a lonely area. "It's certainly away from the center of town."

"I have a feeling no one wants a cemetery near their house."

Jessica giggled nervously as they walked under the sign that said "Pine Hill Cemetery" and stepped onto the path that wove through the grounds. "We shouldn't see much activity here."

"Let's hope not. When I asked Mom this morning where Mr. Laurence is buried, she told me the area it was in and said most of the town came to his funeral here."

Walking from tombstone to tombstone, Jessica said, "Nope . . . Nope . . . Here it is!"

Sophie said, "Harold Laurence. His birth and death dates."

Jessica shuddered. "There's something creepy about being here. It's *very* quiet." A skittering sound to the left made her swing that direction. "A squirrel." She let out a big breath.

Sophie had her hands up to ward off an attack. Jessica coughed to hide her giggle. Her cousin was scared too, and that made Jessica feel much better.

Sophie said, "Let's hurry." She crouched beside the tombstone. "Even up close, there isn't anything on the front other than the words I read."

Jessica walked to the back. "Nothing here. It's

blank." She leaned over the top of the tombstone. "And it's just dirt on top of the grave itself."

Sophie twisted to the side. "You're right. But other graves have grass on top, or there's a stone with words carved in it set in the ground." She rubbed her hand over the grave. "It's loose dirt. I guess rain must have washed dirt over the grave."

Digging her fingers in deeper, she found something hard. "Jessica! There's a flat stone under all this, and I can feel something carved into it."

Jessica hurried around and helped wipe the dirt away.

Both girls sat back on their heels.

Jessica read, "'Wisdom is the key to knowledge.'" She brushed off the edges to make sure there wasn't anything else hidden. "Sophie, this dirt was really fluffy. Rain would make muddy water. Wouldn't it dry hard?"

Sophie nodded. "You're right. That means . . ." She scanned the area. Lowering her voice, she said, "That means someone put dirt here so no one would see these words. They must have thought they were a clue to the treasure."

"People who live here would know what it said."

"Maybe. Maybe not. I doubt most of the people I know in Pine Hill could tell you what's on any of these graves, not unless it was someone close to them."

"You're right." Jessica was surprised to see Sophie glance around nervously before she spoke again.

"Someone came before us, but not long before us,

because it rained a couple of days ago, and they poured fresh dirt all over this."

"They planned it ahead of time because they had a shovel or a bag of dirt."

"That also means we could be making someone nervous, someone who's looking for the treasure and is slightly ahead of us. They're trying to hide clues."

As Jessica stood, movement caught her eye. Something big and black moved behind a stone building. She grabbed Sophie's sleeve and tugged her away from the headstone. "Let's go."

"Huh? I'm not done." Sophie stood.

"Yes. You are. I just saw *someone* hide. Someone wearing black." She pointed to her left.

Sophie looked that way. "It's probably a crow."

"A six-foot-tall crow?"

Sophie stepped back from the stone. "You sure?"

"I know what I saw."

They broke into a run.

Sophie led them to the edge of the city, then slowed down when they were out of breath and well away from the cemetery.

Jessica took in a big gulp of air. She said, "I've been thinking . . . Maybe I saw a plastic tarp or something like that." She played it over and over in her mind. It had looked like a person, but maybe she was wrong. "I *don't* want to have bad guys following us again."

Sophie shook her head. "Me neither. Let's go see Nezzy now. There are lots of houses around her, so we *shouldn't* see anything suspicious."

7

Nezzy's News

The two girls moved more slowly than usual, neither one saying anything. In her heart Jessica felt sure she'd seen someone and that someone had hidden. If so, their mystery had just changed, and not in a good way. Sophie led Jessica up one street, down another, over a path between two large houses, finally stopping in front of a house that sat on a small hill above them.

Jessica looked up. "Wow."

"It's something, isn't it?"

Nezzy Grant's house had wild, crazy things in the design. It was brick, of course; almost everything in Pine Hill—except Sophie's big, white, antique house—was brick. A bright orange flag flew from a turret, purple drapes hung at the sides of a porch that curved around the front of the house, and wooden trim painted blue and yellow added a dizzying element. Jessica knew she wouldn't wear an outfit made up of those colors.

"I remember being here once when Mom needed

to bring something to Mrs. Grant. We stayed outside, but the door stood wide open. Wait until you see inside."

Jessica kept staring at the house. "I'm curious, for sure. Look. There's a large stained glass window that adds even more colors." Turning to Sophie, she said, "I wonder if we should have called first. Even with all of the, uh, unusual details, this is a really fancy place. Another mansion." Jessica pulled out her lip gloss and ran it over her lips, then slipped her fingers through her hair.

"Mrs. Grant came to my church before she got so old, and her housekeeper, Amanda Easton, still does. I'm sure it's fine."

They climbed the steep stairs—brick, as Jessica pointed out—and knocked on the front door.

A woman opened the door. "Well, hello, Sophie. What can I help you with? Are you two selling something?"

"No, ma'am. We wondered if we could speak to Mrs. Grant."

"I'll see." She gestured them inside, then disappeared through a doorway off a long hall.

Standing in the entryway, Jessica couldn't focus on any one thing, there was so much to see. She whispered, "This is a crazy mix. There's a stuffed bird." She pointed toward the ceiling. Turning around to the wall, she said, "And here's a collection of lace."

Sophie whispered, "Maybe this is what Mom meant by eccentric."

As Jessica opened her mouth to speak, Miss Easton entered the room. "She'll see you now." She gestured for them to follow and led them down a long hall and into a large living room with fancy furniture that had lace doilies lying over the back, a totem pole in one corner, a suit of armor in another. Jessica said, "*This* is eccentric."

"Thank you," an old lady's voice came from the corner of the room.

Jessica gulped. "I'm sorry, Mrs. Grant."

The old woman cackled the way Jessica always imagined the witch in "Hansel and Gretel" would right before she got ready to eat the children. "Why ever would I be offended? Please sit down and tell me the reason for your visit."

Sophie and Jessica walked over to her and sat down in red leather chairs.

Sophie said, "My mother thought you could tell us about Mr. Laurence and Hilltop."

Mrs. Grant narrowed her eyes. "April Sandoval sent you, huh?" She leaned back in her chair and rubbed her chin, studying them. "Learned about the treasure, did you?"

Sophie spoke up. "Yes, ma'am."

The woman slapped her knee. "Nezzy."

Both girls jumped.

"Excuse me, ma'am?" Jessica edged back in her chair, away from Mrs. Grant, and tried to keep a happy expression on her face.

"'Ma'am' and 'Mrs. Grant' make me feel old. My

name is Esmeralda, or Nezzy. I don't like that newfangled 'Ms.' thing."

Jessica replied, "Yes, ma'am. I mean Nezzy." The girls looked at each other. It wasn't polite, but it was what she wanted.

Sophie asked, "Did you know old man—I mean, Mr. Laurence?"

Nezzy guffawed. *"Old man Laurence!"*

Sophie nodded slowly. "Yes, ma'a—Nezzy."

Nezzy cackled again. "Get comfortable. I know everything you'd want to about Harold Laurence. *Except* the location of the treasure."

Sophie, her brown eyes sparkling, moved to a chair closer to Nezzy. "There *is* a treasure?"

The old woman got a faraway look in her eyes. "I'm not positive, but I believe there is. The story begins when my family moved to Pine Hill right after I'd turned sixteen. The first day we came to town, I was about to step into the general store when the most handsome man I'd ever seen walked across the street. I was so caught up with watching him that I tripped and fell. He hurried over and helped me up. I really thought I'd marry him, but life can bring unexpected surprises. Mr. Grant moved to Pine Hill the next year and swept me off my feet."

"Was there anything about Mr. Laurence that was unusual?"

Nezzy guffawed again. "Almost everything about that man was unusual. Harold built the mansion about the time he got married, and you know that cost a pretty penny. He started spending money like it was water."

Sophie's eyes grew round and big. "Did he rob banks?"

"Naw. The man I knew wouldn't do anything like that. In the beginning some folks thought that."

"Then where did he get the money?"

Nezzy raised her hands. "I asked him, but he wouldn't say. I always did enjoy talking to that man. Still enjoy going through my memory books."

Jessica tried to pull her back on track. "So people think there's a treasure just because of all the money he had?"

Sophie sat back in her seat and crossed her arms. "That doesn't seem like much of a clue."

"No. There's more to it than that. Many years ago, a man everyone trusted, Doc Jones, said he'd taken a shortcut through the woods in the middle of the night and saw Harold there—with a big bag of gold. There was a bright, full moon that night, and he said it reflected off the open bag and lit it up for him to see clearly."

The girls were silent for a minute.

Sophie said, "Wow. How did Mr. Laurence explain the gold that night when Doc Jones stopped and asked him about it?"

"That's the problem. Doc was hurrying to help someone who was very sick, so he couldn't stop. Harold always said Doc Jones had been mistaken in the dark, that it wasn't him."

"And what about the place where the doctor saw the gold? Could the treasure be hidden there?"

Nezzy shook her head. "Seemed like the whole town went out to look for it. Harold owned that land and more, but he didn't stop anyone from looking."

Jessica glanced out the window. She could see the sun dropping low in the sky. "Sophie, we'd better hurry to Great Finds, or we'll miss the time we told your mother we'd get there."

Sophie turned to the window, then jumped to her feet. "Nezzy, we've really enjoyed our visit."

"Me too, ladies. Please come back. Oh, there is one other thing. Harold's desk was the one piece of furniture that he kept near him as he moved from room to room in that rotting house. When he was nearing the end, he told me, 'The beauty of the desk isn't just skin-deep. It goes deeper than anyone imagines.'" She shook her head. "I've never been sure what that meant." Shrugging, she added, "But it might be a clue to the treasure."

On the way to Great Finds, they passed a building with a poster in the front window and Sophie stopped in her tracks. "Jessica, a carnival's coming to Pine Hill! We haven't had a carnival here since I was a little kid."

"We have a giant Ferris wheel in London called the London Eye, and we go to that every once in a while. Even so, I'd like to go to a carnival. Do you think it will cost a lot?"

"I have a feeling it would take our whole allowance.

And we might need money for things to solve the mystery. Look!" She pointed at the poster. "It's going to be on the grounds of Hilltop to raise money to save the mansion."

"Sophie, I wonder if we should go, just so we can keep our eyes on the house."

"I know what you mean, but they won't let us in for free." Sophie laughed and grabbed Jessica's arm. "We'd better hurry."

When they arrived at Great Finds, Mrs. Sandoval waited just inside the door for them. "I'm ready to close, so I'm glad you're here." She paused with her hand on her purse. "I just remembered that we have company for dinner tonight. I've been so busy today that I forgot. It's a good thing I made lasagna ahead yesterday." She reached into her purse, pulled out some money, and handed it to Sophie. "Girls, please run over to Bananas and get dessert for me."

Going out the door, Sophie asked, "Who's coming over?"

"Huh?" Her mom looked up from the key ring in her hand. "Oh, a couple of people who also want to save Hilltop." She smiled. "After dinner—and dessert—you can stay with us if you want, or you can go out on the porch or to your room so you won't be bored."

Once outside, Sophie said, "I'm for going where we aren't bored."

Jessica laughed. "Me too."

As they stepped into the bakery, Sophie saw Jessica

pause and take a deep breath. In a low voice, her cousin said, "It smells so good in here. Kind of makes you forget that everything Mrs. Bowman bakes has banana in it."

"I know. It's weird, but everything is delicious. And she did try chocolate chip cookies without bananas," Sophie added.

Mrs. Bowman finished up with her customer, then walked over to them. "What do you need today, ladies?"

"Mom sent us over for dessert. We're having company tonight."

"My Triple Berry Cobbler came out especially good today." She pointed at a crumb-topped pan of dessert with a bright berry color around the edges.

Sophie looked over at Jessica, and her cousin's expression seemed to say: *Bananas and berries?!*

Jessica said, "The berry part sounds good. Um, does it have bananas?

Smiling broadly, Mrs. Bowman said. "I tried making it without bananas, but it just didn't taste right. It's wonderful now."

Sophie knew it sounded strange, but it would probably be delicious. "Sounds good to me."

Jessica seemed a little less certain.

The older woman pulled the foil pan of cobbler out of the glass case and reached for one of her yellow boxes. "Is anyone I know coming to dinner?"

"Mom said she'd invited a couple of people." Just then, an idea popped into Sophie's head. Mrs.

Bowman probably knew everyone in town. "Does Mr. Jenkins come in here?"

"Oh my, yes. He's such a nice man. He's been wonderful to my sister. So kind." Mrs. Bowman tucked the pan into the box and started folding the sides in.

"Why is he wonderful?" Sophie asked.

"Emma Jean retired from teaching a few years ago, so she had extra time in her day. She offered to clean the old Laurence mansion for free to help out the city. Every Thursday and Saturday she spends a couple of hours there cleaning the safe areas, the ones that are in decent shape. Mr. Jenkins kindly said she didn't need to clean the area he sleeps in, and that saves her a lot of time. She says he always has a smile for her and insists that she not bother with his rooms." Mrs. Bowman set the box on the counter.

Sophie paid her. "He does sound nice."

As she walked to the cash register, Mrs. Bowman said, "He asked about you two the other day when he bought some muffins. Banana chocolate chip."

"Really?" Jessica asked.

"Yes, they're my personal favorite muffin. I love the chocolate scattered through them."

Jessica blinked.

Sophie knew that wasn't what she'd meant.

Jessica said, "I'm sure they're delicious. What did Mr. Jenkins want to know?"

"He'd heard about the mystery you solved and wondered if I knew more about what had happened. I guess he asked because everyone knows I helped you."

Sophie put her hand over her mouth to hide her grin. "Helped" probably wasn't the right word. Mrs. Bowman never learned that she'd been one of their suspects in the last mystery.

As the older woman handed Sophie her change, another customer walked in the door.

"What did you tell him?" Sophie asked quickly.

"I told him you were great detectives. I thought that would make him happy, but it didn't seem to."

As they left the bakery, Jessica said, "Everyone seems to love Mr. Jenkins. That was odd that he asked about us though."

Sophie thought about it. "It is, but we haven't heard anyone say anything bad about him." She shifted the box in her arms. "I doubt there's anything suspicious about him."

8

Noises in the Night

A *clunk* woke Jessica.

Clunk again. Had someone broken into the house?

Another sound came from the wall on the other side of the bedroom, this one more like tapping. Tapping, tapping. Heart racing, Jessica turned toward Sophie's bed. She gulped. Sophie wasn't there. Knowing Sophie, she'd woken up and gone to check out the source of the noise that Jessica thought came through the wall from Aunt April's office.

Jessica reached for her phone. The off-and-on reception in Pine Hill might make it iffy for calling people, but it still told the time: *2 a.m.* She silently slipped out of bed and crept out the door, which had been left partway open by Sophie, or whoever had snuck into the house.

When the tapping stopped, Jessica froze. After a minute, she continued toward her aunt's office, which she was confident was the source of the noise. She found the door shut, so she gently turned the knob and pushed it open an inch. Someone sat on the floor next to the desk, almost out of sight from where Jessica stood. The person turned, and she saw who it was. "Sophie!"

Her cousin jumped about six inches in the air. "Ooh, you scared me!"

"*I* scared *you*? I was scared stiff when I woke up and heard strange sounds. Then you were gone . . ."

Sophie hurried over and pushed the door shut, turning the knob as gently to close it as Jessica had to open it. "I couldn't sleep. I kept thinking about the key. It has to fit something in the desk. Help me?"

Jessica rolled her eyes. "Sure. Why not? I can't think of a thing I'd rather be doing in the middle of the night. Other than maybe sleeping. But if I help you, we might both be able to go back to sleep. You have one hour."

"Deal."

Jessica crouched beside the desk, with Sophie kneeling beside her. "You know, there probably isn't anything else hidden in this desk. I suspect Mr. Laurence was just old and meant to put a different key in the envelope."

"Think about what he told Nezzy about the desk. All we found was a photo. That doesn't seem worth mentioning to her."

"It's definitely not the treasure people have talked about for close to a hundred years."

Sophie's eyes got big. "Sooo, you agree there may be something else hidden in the desk."

Jessica shrugged. "Maybe. Now that I'm up, let's look for it. What now, O wise one?"

Sophie stood. "Let's start with what we know." She pointed at the side with the hidden drawer.

Jessica reached inside and pushed first the button to open the large drawer and then the button inside it to cause it to swing to the side.

"We stopped examining the desk when we found the hidden drawers. What if they were just the easiest hidden places to find?"

"It seemed like there should be drawers. I think that makes them something people would look for."

"*Very true.*" Sophie studied the desk.

Jessica crouched at the side of the desk and ran her hand underneath the bottom edge. "I'll pick up where I left off."

"Me too." Sophie rolled the top back and leaned over the front of the desk.

They worked without speaking for a while. Then Jessica said, "We should have gone to the library and searched on the computer for 'desks with hidden compartments.' We might have gotten some ideas about where to look and saved some time."

"I wonder . . . No, I don't think Dad would be happy if we went into his office in the middle of the night."

A man's voice said, "He wouldn't be happy if you woke him up either."

Mr. Sandoval stood in the doorway with a metal fireplace poker in his right hand and a flashlight in his left.

Jessica leaned against the wall, hand on her heart.

"You scared us, Dad!" Sophie said.

He glared at them. "How do you think I felt when I heard tapping in the night?"

"Um, maybe this wasn't my best idea?"

"Now you're thinking right." He pointed at the desk. "What's going on?"

Sophie said, "We—"

Jessica cleared her throat.

"Okay. *I* decided to see if there were more hidden compartments in the desk."

"Uh-huh. And?"

"Nothing so far. Would you like to help?"

Mr. Sandoval seemed to fight a battle with himself, first looking annoyed and then interested. He finally grinned and set down the fireplace poker. "I wouldn't miss it. Let's try to keep it down so we don't wake up your mom. No more tapping, okay?"

Both girls nodded.

Inside, across the back of the desk there were three rows of small storage places: two rows of open boxes big enough to hold a letter or two—cubbyholes, her aunt had called them—and under those, a row of tiny drawers that could hold a handful of paper clips each. Between each drawer there was a round piece of metal for decoration. Sophie peered first into the cubbyholes. "Hold your flashlight here, Dad." She pointed at the spot.

Jessica stopped what she was doing to watch. "Find something?"

"Maybe." Sophie groaned when her dad shined the light into the box. "Dirt. It's just dirt on the back of a cubbyhole."

Jessica giggled. "It's probably antique dirt."

"Maybe Mom would like it." Sophie grinned.

Mr. Sandoval chuckled. "She might. You know, we could be on an impossible mission. Consider all of the people who have looked for the treasure for more than a hundred years."

"And not found it," Jessica added.

Sophie pulled out a tiny drawer and peered into the hole it left. "None of them were friends with Mr. Laurence."

"I think *every* one of his friends would have looked for the treasure," Mr. Sandoval said.

"You may be right. There's something about the word 'treasure' that gets people excited. But Nezzy had special information. He told her the desk was important."

Sophie bent over the side of the desk. "Whoa!"

"What?" Jessica crowded next to her.

"When I looked at the hole from the side, I noticed that the metal decoration between these two drawers looks like a button, not just a pretty decoration."

"And?" Jessica stood.

"Let's see." Jessica stood on one side of her and Mr. Sandoval on the other, both leaning in as Sophie pushed the piece of metal. The tiny drawer swung sideways to reveal a hidden cubbyhole behind it.

Jessica leaned over the side of the desk. "Wow!"

Sophie reached her hand into the hole. "*Nothing.* I was *so* sure . . . I'm starting to wonder about the treasure myself."

"Let me check. There must be more." Jessica nudged Sophie to the side and put her hand inside the hole. "Hey, the bottom is loose!" She pushed on it, flipping the end of the board up so she could lift it out. When her uncle shone the light inside, she craned her neck to peer into it. "Empty! This is so frustrating. I really thought we'd found something."

Mr. Sandoval said, "Let me see." Jessica stepped aside and he handed the flashlight to Sophie. "What about the little drawer at the back of the hole?"

The girls leaned in. He reached inside and slid out a tiny drawer.

Sophie groaned. "Nothing! There should be a law that secret compartments must have something great inside." She lifted it from her dad's hand and turned it upside down. "There isn't anything underneath either."

"Maybe . . ." Sophie reached inside and flipped up a board under the new drawer. "There are layers upon layers of hidden places in this desk." Bouncing with excitement, Sophie reached her hand inside. "I feel like we're close to a big discovery." Then she sighed and pulled her hand out. "Nothing."

Jessica stepped back and studied the desk. "You know, Sophie, if this drawer on the left side of the desk has all of this, the drawer in the same place on the right might too."

Sophie smacked her head. "Obvious. My detective brain cells must be asleep."

"Perfectly reasonable since it's the middle of the night," Jessica muttered.

Mr. Sandoval chuckled. "If there isn't anything here, we'll need to go back to bed and try another time. During daylight hours."

Sophie focused intently on the desk. She pushed the center of the medallion between the two drawers on the right, watched as the drawer swung out, this time designed with a glass jar in the center. Sophie said, "I've seen something like this before. Mom told me it would have had ink in the jar before modern pens, from when people wrote with pens they dipped into ink."

Jessica reached inside the open compartment and flipped up the bottom board. Then she reached inside to open the little drawer. "It's stuck."

Mr. Sandoval shone the light into the slot so she could see better. "Should I get a tool to help open it?"

When Sophie peered inside, her jaw dropped. "This drawer has a keyhole." She reached into her robe pocket and pulled out a key. "I brought it just in case." She fit her hand inside the hole. "You couldn't have a large hand and do this. Everyone ready?" She looked up at her dad and Jessica. After a few seconds, she whispered, "It fits."

Sophie slid the drawer out and they peered into the tiny, empty space.

Mr. Sandoval groaned. "I thought you'd found

something. Well, we'd better all head back to bed. Morning will come quickly."

"Just a sec, Dad. We should see if there's a space under the drawer, like on the other side. This one was locked, so maybe it's more important."

Jessica reached in and flipped out the board. "Yep." She reached her hand into the hole and hit something cold and metallic. She ran her fingers over it, feeling the outline of the object. "Not again!"

Mr. Sandoval asked, "Jessica, are you okay?"

She wrapped her fingers around the object, slid her hand out, and held up a large key.

Instead of looking frustrated, Sophie's eyes gleamed with excitement.

Jessica raised both hands in exasperation. "Now we have to find something else with a keyhole."

Mr. Sandoval said, "Since this is a larger key, my guess is that your treasure hunt just took a turn away from the desk."

Jessica dangled the key by the end. "You're right, Uncle Lucas. This is a different kind of key. And it's kind of pretty, like keys were a long time ago."

Sophie lifted it from Jessica's hand. "Maybe this time when we find the place the key fits, we'll also find the treasure."

9

Hilltop Tour

Sophie fought a yawn as she watched Jessica dry and style her blonde hair, then put on makeup. It was so much work *every single day*. After wondering for just a second if she should give it a try, she quickly shifted her mind to their mystery and went through their clues. Everything came back to Hilltop. An idea popped into her mind. She'd be extra helpful at Great Finds. *Then* she'd ask her mother to help them get into Hilltop.

They walked into town and to her mother's shop.

When Sophie found her mother with no customers, she put her plan into play. "Do you need us to do anything, Mom?" Sophie made herself smile broadly.

Mrs. Sandoval picked up her mug of coffee and peered over the rim as she took a sip. "You must want a favor."

"Wellll . . ."

So much for sneaking up on her mother with the idea.

"I'll take you up on your offer later. Right now, I have good news for you. Your father talked to Mr. Jenkins about letting you see Hilltop."

Sophie froze. There could be a clue in the house. Would they find the treasure today? "And?"

"He said you could come over today."

Sophie felt a real smile spread over her face. "Are you or Dad coming with us?"

"Neither. Emma Jean Walker is going to be cleaning there today. Your father and I have known her for years."

"That's great!"

"Try not to pester Mr. Jenkins with your questions. Also, remember that Hilltop may belong to the city, but it's his home right now. Think of it like a museum. Don't touch anything."

"Mom! How can I investigate if I can't touch *anything*?"

Her mom paused. "I'll revise that. Touch, but be very careful not to break."

Sophie nodded. "Deal."

"When are we scheduled to go?" Jessica asked.

"I'll run you over right now. I want to make sure Emma Jean is there."

Jessica left the room to brush her hair.

As Sophie watched her cousin leave, she felt less girly than she thought she should. Leaning close to her mother, she said, "Mom, would it be okay if I wore makeup?"

Her mother reared back. "What?"

Sophie watched her but didn't say anything else.

"I want you to wait to wear makeup."

"But Jessica—"

"That's between her and her parents." Mrs. Sandoval rearranged teacups on a shelf. "I'm willing to let you wear a very light pink lip gloss, but that's all."

"Thanks, Mom." Sophie reached up and hugged her.

As Mrs. Sandoval drove, Jessica pictured the Laurence house. "There are some very large holes in the roof, and I suspect some large rodents have decided to call it home."

Sophie laughed. "Just be ready to run if any rats come out to meet us."

Mrs. Sandoval gazed up at the sky. "The forecast said we could get some severe thunderstorms today. Be careful when you're out."

"We will, Mom."

When they turned onto Hilltop's driveway, the car dipped into a big rut and bounced. Jessica grabbed the door handle and held on. "The road seemed bad when we were walking." Her voice vibrated on the rough spots. "But it's a bumpy mess in a car."

When they arrived at the front of the house, Jessica gladly got out. "Whew! I'm happy we're walking home."

"Me too!" Sophie stepped out and shut the door.

As her aunt climbed out of the car, she studied the sky. "The clouds are getting darker. Sophie, I want you to promise me that you two won't go outside if there is thunder or lightning."

"Sure, Mom. Why so serious?"

"There are a lot of trees here, and they're a magnet for lightning. Stay here until the storm passes. Jessica?"

"Yes, Aunt April."

Jessica was happy when Miss Walker greeted them at the front door since they couldn't go in if she wasn't there. They stood inside the entry as her aunt waved and climbed back into her car. Miss Walker waited beside them while Mrs. Sandoval drove away. Then she said, "Girls, I'll be working in the house, but never far away if you need me."

When she reached over to dust a table beside her— she must not like dust to be anywhere—Sophie leaned over and whispered to Jessica, "I have the weirdest sense that maybe we should have asked Mom to stay."

Thunder, lightning, and a house even Jessica had to admit was more than a little creepy didn't make her excited to see that car go down the driveway either. Even she had to wonder if it was right to be here. Jessica pulled out the photo of the house. It still amazed her that this used to be a fabulous place.

At that moment Mr. Jenkins stepped into the entryway with a big smile on his face.

Jessica tucked the photo back into her purse. "Aunt April said we could see the inside of the house. Is that possible?"

"I'm happy to show around someone who's

interested in this old place." Turning toward Miss Walker, Mr. Jenkins said, "Emma Jean, go ahead and start in the kitchen. I'm going to give these two a tour."

Miss Walker bent over and reached into a bag that had paper towels and cleaning supplies sticking out of it, rifled through it, and stood back up. She said, "I stopped for supplies this morning but just realized I missed one thing. Mr. Jenkins, please let me know when Sophie and Jessica leave. I'll need to run to the store." She added, "These are smart girls, so don't leave out anything interesting." She went through the door.

He said, "Girls, I want to warn you: the house is in terrible condition. Old Mr. Laurence let it run down around him. He just kept moving his bed and desk to an area that was livable and dry. Then he moved again when that one deteriorated."

Jessica turned in a circle. A dusty crystal chandelier hung from the two-story ceiling over a staircase that split at a landing in the middle, curving elegantly to the right and left. Floors in the entry were what looked to be gray and white marble, Jessica guessed, but they were too grimy to tell. This must have been a beautiful house when it was new and when it was clean.

"I thought Miss Walker cleaned the house."

Mr. Jenkins frowned. "The city told her to only clean the areas I actually use. They said they didn't want to take advantage of her kindness by having her clean a building they may tear down." He ushered them on. "I'll show you where the old man lived."

They followed him past a closed door and down a hallway with vacant spaces on the walls from pictures, the dust and discolored paint around them leaving ghosts of what once hung there. A room with a large desk and dark wood-covered walls lined with book-shelves, all in good condition, sat to the left.

"My office," he said, pointing as they kept walking.

Jessica asked, "What happened to the paintings that used to hang on the walls?"

"Mr. Laurence had to sell them," Jenkins said glumly. "He sold most things of value in this old house to pay bills."

They entered a bedroom, or at least a room that had a bed in it.

"This was the family's informal dining room before the old man moved in here."

"Why here?" Sophie asked.

"His bedroom had always been on the second floor, but the condition of the upstairs got worse and worse. The roof leaked and some windows wouldn't close right. Mr. Laurence also had more and more trouble climbing the stairs. He decided to move to a part of the house that was in good shape and on the ground floor."

Sophie asked, "Where do you live?"

"I live in the basement," he said. "There are old servants' quarters next to a shop of sorts where things were made and repaired. It's warm and mostly dry."

The girls checked out Harold Laurence's room. There wasn't much furniture, just a twin bed, a small dresser, and what must have been a comfy chair, but now had a rip across the seat and stuffing coming out of one arm. Wallpaper with green and pink flowers had peeled off about half the walls. A cleared area in the corner looked like the only space large enough for the desk at Sophie's house.

Seeming to read her mind, Mr. Jenkins said, "The desk Sophie's mother has in her shop was there." He pointed to the spot Jessica had noticed.

Neither girl corrected him about the location of the desk. Jessica figured it would probably go back to the shop eventually anyway.

"I can answer any questions you have. Let's go to the front parlor." He led them back down the hall and opened the door they'd walked by before. The parlor was filled with dining room furniture.

"I helped him sell whatever he didn't use. The parlor's furniture was the most valuable, and he didn't leave his room in the last years, so he didn't need it. Once it was gone, I moved the dining room furniture from his bedroom space in here so visitors would have somewhere to sit other than the kitchen table."

The phone rang just as everyone had taken seats at the dining room table on worn, faded green velvet seats that matched the wallpaper in Harold Laurence's last bedroom. Mr. Jenkins stood, saying, "If you'll excuse me, I've been expecting a business call and will take it in the office." He hurried down the hall they'd just come down and Jessica heard a door close behind him.

As soon as he'd left the room, Sophie said in a low voice, "I want to check out Harold Laurence's room when Mr. Jenkins isn't there so he doesn't wonder what's going on. Maybe he left a clue there."

Jessica bit her lip. "I'd like to see too, but someone should stay here." She waved her arm at the room.

"Agreed." Sophie stood and started to walk away.

"Hurry!" Jessica said in a hushed voice. "He might be back in a few seconds." She watched Sophie disappear down the hall.

Jessica arose from her seat and nervously wandered around the room, stopping at the fireplace to pick up each figurine on the mantel to check it out— for what, she didn't know. They must not have been valuable anyway since they were still here. Another empty rectangle over the fireplace told her a picture had been sold. Knowing Mr. Jenkins would be coming back soon, she sat back down, but then stood again and pulled out her phone. *Photos of the inside of the house might be important later.*

She raced around the room, snapping pictures, then stepped out into the entrance and hurried down the hall, pausing every few seconds to take a shot. Knowing she'd been taking a chance on how long Mr. Jenkins would be gone, Jessica raced back to the dining room and stood next to her chair. Tapping her fingers on the table nervously, she wondered where Sophie was. Peering around the corner of the doorway, she saw Sophie stopped in front of the office door.

Jessica waved her over, but Sophie didn't seem to see her. Her cousin leaned against the office door, her eyes getting bigger as she did so. Then Sophie hurried over to a chair, slid into it, and pointed at Jessica's chair. Jessica sat only seconds before a smiling Mr. Jenkins walked into the room.

"Sorry, ladies. Just a small problem with my dear old mother's car."

"No problem, Mr. Jenkins." Sophie stood. "I think we've learned enough today, don't you, Jessica?"

Jessica reared backward. They'd had a tour but hadn't asked any questions. And they certainly hadn't told him about the hidden compartment in the desk.

Sophie continued smiling. "Thank you for your time. We can see ourselves to the door." And without another word, she turned and left the parlor, Jessica on her heels, and closed the door to that room behind her.

Jessica followed her to the front door. She whispered, "What's going on?"

Sophie put her finger to her lips. "Shh."

"Sophie, what's going on?"

"I don't know. But I can tell you that Jim Jenkins isn't who he's pretending to be."

As she opened the big, old door, thunder crashed overhead.

10

Hide-and-Seek

Jessica had known something wasn't right when Sophie glanced back toward the closed parlor door with a spooked expression on her face. Sophie hurried out the front door, and Jessica stayed on her heels. Another, louder clap of thunder sounded, followed quickly by lightning streaking across the sky.

They whirled back around and into the house. Sophie pulled Jessica away from the entrance to the parlor and whispered, "As I walked by Mr. Jenkins' office, I heard him speaking in an angry way. I thought, *That's weird, because he seems like such a nice man.*

"When I leaned against the door, I heard him say, 'Yeah, Lester, I hear you, but get off my back. I'm good for it.' Lester must have talked then, because it was quiet. Then Mr. Jenkins said, 'The old man was loaded. I'll get my share.'"

Jessica whispered back, "Wow! Now I see why you wanted to leave."

"But we can't. I promised Mom we'd stay inside if a storm struck."

"Miss Walker is working here. Maybe we should go find her."

"Good idea!"

Just then, a little gray car drove by the window.

"Uh-oh. Mr. Jenkins must have told her we'd left."

Lightning lit up the sky again. "It's getting worse out there. I know I have to keep my promise to Mom." Sophie's breathing quickened. "I also know we shouldn't stay right here."

Jessica pointed through the doorway of the room in front of them. "Maybe we can stay *here*. It's filthy, so he probably doesn't even come into this room. Then when the storm's gone, we'll quietly leave."

Sophie glanced over her shoulder. "Maybe he won't know we were here."

"Exactly."

When they entered the room, Jessica discovered that it had a cracked window, and it looked like an animal had built a nest in the corner. "I don't think this room is on any tours."

Sophie looked around. "Me neither. Even Miss Walker has abandoned it. I'm going to go through the door on the other side of the room. Maybe it's a better place to be." Sophie slowly opened the door. "It's a butler's pantry, and the kitchen's next to it."

"A what?"

"A small room between the kitchen and dining room. I've seen them in other old houses Mom's taken me to. I guess that in the old days it was a place where a butler worked on things he was about to take into the dining room."

When they went through into the kitchen, Jessica felt a lot safer. Speaking in a normal voice, she said, "This is clean and seems like a nice, safe place to wait. I doubt Mr. Jenkins comes here very often."

Sophie pulled the old-fashioned ruffled curtains shut, closed the door that opened to the hallway, and both girls sat at the small, round kitchen table.

Jessica nervously rubbed her hands together. "Do you think Mr. Jenkins is dangerous?"

Sophie pursed her lips. "I don't know. He seems so nice. Everyone thinks he's nice."

"I assumed he was just as nice as everyone thought, even Tony. Then you overheard his conversation. Are you sure you heard the words clearly?"

"Yes. And I don't think 'Lester' is someone I'd like to meet."

A shadow passed by the curtain. "I'm glad Miss Walker is back."

"Me too!"

A knock on the door made them both jump. Jessica whispered, "*Not* Miss Walker. She has a key." A louder knock made Jessica jump again.

"That's going to bring Mr. Jenkins here in a hurry!" Sophie dropped to her knees. "We need somewhere to hide. There are two doors we haven't opened. You try that one"—Sophie pointed—"and I'll try the other. Stay low."

They crab-walked across the room, and Jessica pulled a door open. "Pantry. We could hide in the corner."

Sophie tried hers. "Stairs to the basement. Let's go." She was halfway down the stairs before Jessica could even decide what to do.

Jessica had stepped through the basement door and almost pulled it closed when Mr. Jenkins came into the kitchen and opened the door to the outside.

"Lester! What a pleasant surprise." Jessica could tell by his voice that the visit was less than pleasant.

When the men walked out of the room, Jessica pulled the door closed the rest of the way and went down the stairs. "Sophie," she whispered. "Sophie!" she said a little louder.

"Over here." Sophie stepped out of the shadows in the corner of the room. "I wanted to see if we had a way out of here, so I checked out every room, including Mr. Jenkins'." She glanced back to those shadows. "Tell me what you think about what I found."

"Sophie, we shouldn't invade his privacy. It's his room."

"The whole house belongs to the city, and this is important. Follow me."

Sophie led her through the shadows, opened a door, and they stepped into a fully furnished room. Sophie closed the door as Jessica turned in a circle, checking it all out. Paintings hung on the walls, and what appeared to be other treasures sat on shelves.

Jessica said, "Why would these things be here? Mr.

Jenkins said he'd helped Mr. Laurence sell everything of value."

"That what I thought! He kept these and hid them in his room."

Jessica examined several of the paintings. "Sophie, I think at least some of these are worth a lot. They remind me of things I've seen in museums."

Sophie opened the door and peered out. "Let's get out of here. We don't know when he might come downstairs."

Jessica had just closed the door behind her when the one at the top of the stairs opened. The girls ducked into the shadowy corner. Jessica hid as far in the corner as she could fit. She bit her lip so she wouldn't yell out loud when she leaned against a rough brick, and stayed there as still as she could.

"Lester, I tell you I've got the money covered. I can lay my hands on a lot of cash in a hurry."

Lester almost growled when he said, "Then do it! I want my money now. Turn on another light, Jenkins. It's dark in here."

Sophie grabbed Jessica's arm. They'd be discovered if he turned on a bright light!

"That tiny light hanging from the ceiling is the only one that's electric, and the old gaslights don't work anymore. Old man Laurence never spent money in this part of the house." He sounded very pleased with himself when he added, "I wired my room and connected it to the electric box so it's well-lit and warm."

The door to his room opened, and he flipped on the light.

"This stuff must be worth a bundle. Sell it and give me my money."

"I've been holding on to all of this, the best of what the old man had, until I know it's safe to sell. Most of these artists are so well-known that someone might notice the sale, and I'd end up behind bars."

Lester chuckled. "Wouldn't be the first time."

"I'm never going back. I play it safe now. I'll pay you when I find the treasure."

"Right. You're going to find what no one else has. I know better men than you that tried."

"None of them were inside the house. I have access to every clue the old man left."

"What if someone else finds it first?"

"Everyone else seems to have given up. Except a couple of girls." He started to close the door. "And if they get in my way—"

The door cut off the rest of his words.

Jessica rose on shaky legs. She pointed to the stairs and moved as softly—but as quickly—as she could up them and out the door, with Sophie on her heels. When she opened the kitchen door, she saw Miss Walker drive around the corner and park. Jessica almost waved to her, then realized she might accidentally say something to Mr. Jenkins that would give away the fact that they hadn't left earlier, and that could be very bad for them.

After pulling the door closed, Jessica tugged Sophie

into the hall and both girls raced toward the front door. Sophie passed her in the hall and opened the door. The weather had been so bad that no visitors were out there, so they closed the door behind them and ran unnoticed down the drive.

When they were out of sight of the house, Jessica stopped, leaning forward and panting. "The storm seems to have passed." She pointed up to patches of blue sky peeking out between the clouds.

"Jessica, we've got bigger problems than thunder and lightning."

11

Hidden Trail

Sophie thought trouble had followed them when she heard gravel crunching. Jessica had reached down to retie her shoes so she didn't seem to notice. Sophie waved her arms to get her attention, then put her fingers over her own lips to tell Jessica to be quiet when she opened her mouth to speak.

Gravel crunched again. She grabbed Jessica's arm, pulled her into the woods, and pushed her behind a boulder. Someone laughed and Sophie started to relax. When a little kid squealed, she knew it was a family and gave a big sigh of relief. Definitely not bad guys.

Both girls stood.

Sophie really looked around them for the first time. "Jessica, there's an old trail here. I wonder where it goes."

"What trail? I just see bushes and trees."

"Here." Sophie pointed at the ground. "It's a little overgrown."

Jessica slowly shook her head from side to side. "A little? I missed it completely."

Sophie pushed a branch aside. "Let's check it out. This must have been a path in the olden days. Maybe there's a clue at the end of it."

"And maybe there are only snakes and other creepy things."

Sophie grabbed the back of Jessica's shirt when she started down the trail, and held her still. "Just don't touch anything I didn't touch."

Jessica looked at her in confusion, so she added, "Poison ivy. This might be a trail that was used more in the past, but it's rarely used by humans these days. I think it's a game trail now."

"A what?"

"A trail deer and other animals use. See how it used to be a lot wider?" She pointed at the edge of the trail. "There are scruffy weeds and grass now but no trees have grown in."

"I wonder if it was used more when Mr. Laurence was younger."

"He might have walked here often if it was a special place."

"And he might have buried treasure in a special place."

"Uh-huh."

After they'd walked about five minutes on a trail that turned and wove through the trees, Jessica said, "This makes Cutoff Trail look good. At least the bushes and bugs weren't crowded around me."

They stopped at a fork in the trail. "Which way, Sophie?"

Sophie pointed to the right as if she knew the way, but she wasn't sure. She didn't want to admit it, but taking this path might not have been her best idea. Every step took them farther away from the road into an unknown she might have trouble backing her way out of. They passed two trees that had grown twisted together. "This is unusual, so we can remember it, if we get lost."

"Are we going to get lost?"

"No one knows they're going to get lost, or they wouldn't do it."

Jessica glared at her.

Sophie pushed aside a tree's branches and a flock of birds exploded into the air.

Jessica clutched her hand to her chest. "That's it. If we don't find civilization in the next two minutes, we're turning around."

Sophie gulped. She wasn't sure she could get them back to the road. She pushed through the trees and stepped into a clearing, or at least what had been a clearing in the past. Grass stood about a foot tall and would be much taller later in the summer.

Jessica stepped beside her. "I'm sorry I doubted you."

"I was actually getting a little, um, concerned, myself."

Jessica rubbed her arms nervously. "I'm glad I wasn't alone on that."

Shifting bushes caught Sophie's eye. She whispered, "I see something moving. Over there." She pointed toward a clump of trees.

A deer stepped out from the trees, saw the two of them, and flicked its tail in the air before running off through the woods.

Jessica's voice shook when she said, "I need peace and calm. Two mysteries so close together have made me edgy." She looked down just then and stared at her arm.

"Is something wrong?"

Jessica moved her arm so Sophie could see it. A key about the size of a candy bar was imprinted on it.

Sophie reached out and touched the red mark. "How did you get this?"

Jessica shook her head. "I don't know. Wait! I do know. I was pressed against a rough brick when we hid in the basement. The brick must have had the key design on it."

Sophie shook her head in amazement. "Jessica, this may be a clue."

Jessica rubbed her arm. "It's already starting to fade away. How do we get back into the basement to search?"

"Let's figure that out when we're done here." Sophie motioned around them. "We're near Hilltop right now, maybe even on Hilltop's land, so let's examine everything here very carefully." Sophie started around the clearing. "And be careful of plants with three leaves together. It's probably poison ivy."

They both explored. Jessica stopped for quite a while at a tall, skinny bush, so Sophie walked over to see what she'd found.

Jessica pointed. "I thought this was a big bush at first, but it was funny-shaped. Look closely." Stone peeked out between the green leaves.

Sophie squatted down to see the bottom of it. "It's an old fireplace and chimney!" She tugged at the vines.

Turning in a circle, Sophie said, "I'm guessing this was a cabin that burned down. Look: there are stones that make the edge of it, and there are some scattered on the ground." She stopped and stepped inside the remains of the old cabin. "Maybe we should check under each of the stones."

"That would be *so* much work." Jessica glared at them. "But I just remembered what Lenny and Mr. Jenkins said about us. If we find the treasure, maybe they'll move away. On second thought, I'd be happy to check those stones."

Sophie turned away from her cousin, who now crouched on the ground and pushed stones back one by one. Starting on the chimney, Sophie checked each of the stones.

A half hour later, Jessica stood and groaned. "My legs are aching. I don't know if this is helping, Sophie. Anything over there?"

Sophie stepped to the side of the chimney. "I've pushed on about half of the stones here, hoping one is loose and hiding something."

Jessica moved over to the chimney. "Walking feels so good." She bent to her right side and stretched one leg, then the other. "Did you check inside the chimney to see if there was anything odd?"

Sophie moved around in front of it. "I think the only thing that would be odd is if I stuck my head up a chimney."

"Still . . ."

Sophie sat down and scooted backward into the fireplace. "You know, this is so big that I can almost stand up." As she tried to do that, a storm of dirt, leaves, and soot poured down and out.

Coughing, Jessica ran about ten feet away. When the dust settled, she asked quietly, "Sophie, are you okay?"

Sophie crab-walked out of the fireplace, covered in debris, but with her shirt pulled up over her face. "I felt it starting, so I made sure I'd be able to breathe. I feel okay."

Jessica came over to her and pulled an eggshell off her head. "I think a bird must have made a nest in the chimney." Jessica cleared her throat to hide the laughter that tried to bubble up.

Sophie saw the shell and started giggling. Standing, she stretched. "I don't think we'll find any clues in this chimney. Let's see if there's anything else in the clearing." Sophie reached down and picked up a couple of skinny tree branches from the ground. "Lift branches up with this. Oh, and, be careful of anything that moves."

"Because . . ."

"There could be snakes."

Jessica froze with one foot in the air. "Now you tell me?"

"Well, they like to lie in the sun, and the sun's coming out."

"Just call me Wilderness Woman." She took a stick from Sophie and walked around the clearing.

Sophie could hardly believe her eyes. "Why aren't you running away?"

Jessica kept working. "I hate to admit it, but I want to know if there's something here that will help us solve the mystery and find the treasure."

Sophie laughed. "I've got you hooked." She leaned over and poked around in the weeds with her stick.

"I know I want to find the treasure, if there is a treasure, before Mr. Jenkins does."

Sophie said, "Ouch!" and rubbed her knees. "My legs hit . . . I don't know what." She used her stick to pull aside bushes and weeds. Stones like those in the fireplace were stacked on top of each other and formed a circle with a hole in the center.

"It's a well. I saw one at an old house in England."

"Let's clear the area to look for anything that's unusual about the well." Sophie held a bush up on her stick. "This is strange. These bushes seem to be dead, like someone piled them here."

They both reached in and swiped at everything with their sticks. When they'd cleared it all away, they walked around the circular well.

Sophie leaned over the well's opening. "It's deep."

"Be careful, Cousin!" Jessica held on to the back of her shirt.

"I'm okay." Sophie picked up a small rock from the ground and dropped it in. A splash came seconds later. "It sounds deep."

Jessica knelt at the side of the well. "I thought it would be made of rough stones, but it's kind of pretty. The stones are smooth. Here's one with a key on it. Mr. Laurence did love keys."

"What if it's a clue, Jessica?"

"It's a rock in the side of a well. I don't plan to go down in the well to see if something's hidden there."

Sophie thought about the wet, dark hole she'd tossed the rock into. "I don't think I do either." Dropping her stick, she said, "We should head back now, before Mom has a chance to worry."

"Definitely. I think we've panicked and worried enough for all of Pine Hill today."

"You got that right." Sophie studied the area around them. She didn't want to add to Jessica's worry, but she wasn't sure where they were.

Jessica watched her. "Uh-oh. You don't know how to get us out of here."

Sophie made herself smile. "Sure, I do. We can go back the way we came. But I'm not loving the idea of getting that close to the mansion again today."

"Me neither."

Sophie circled the clearing and found another trail, maybe the same trail, as it kept going into Pine Hill.

"There's a path heading this way, and I think that's the way to town." She pointed. "The good news is that if I guessed wrong, we'll probably find the lake and know to go the other way."

"That is good news. Well, your woods skills are better than mine, since those are nonexistent, so you lead and I'll follow."

Sophie chose a trail and they went down it for a while. Then she went to the left at a fork in the trail and they followed it for a few minutes. Feeling as if she'd led them deeper into the woods instead of closer to town, she stopped, a panicky feeling working its way up her body.

"You're lost, right?" Jessica asked.

"Maybe just a little bit." Sophie held her thumb and forefinger close together.

"If we had a hill to climb, maybe we could see around us."

Sophie snapped her fingers. "Of course, I should have thought of finding a high point. I'll climb a tree." Staring up into the trees around them, she chose one with a heavy branch low to the ground. Moving over to the base of it, she climbed onto it and worked her way up the tree. Just over the height of Jessica's head, she could see beyond them to the lake.

Sophie pointed. "It's like I said. I can see the lake, so I know we go that way"—she pointed to her right— "to get to town."

"I'm very glad to hear those words. I've had enough excitement for one day."

12

Sharing Suspicions

Fifteen minutes later, the girls could see the town. Sophie was more relieved than she'd expected to be. There were people here. "I may normally like being in nature, but I'm happy to see buildings right now."

"I am too. I've been thinking as we walked. We should tell Sheriff Valeska what happened at Hilltop."

Sophie sighed. "You're right. Part of me doesn't want to because she'll probably say she can't do anything about it and that we may have misunderstood his words."

"Part of *me* agrees with you, Sophie. The other part thinks we'd better tell her so she knows Mr. Jenkins may not be as nice as everyone says."

"Right."

They went down Main Street, then stood across the street from the sheriff's office for a minute. "I say we go in, Jessica. You with me?"

Jessica nodded once. "I'm with you."

Sophie said, "I don't think there's any point in

telling her about the desk. We don't know if it matters."

"Agreed. We stick to what just happened."

When they stepped inside, they were greeted by the new secretary, Clare Morton, who hadn't looked happy to see them the few times they'd stopped by since she'd taken the job.

Sheriff Valeska called out from her desk. "Can I help you ladies?"

Sophie and Jessica looked at each other, then went over and sat down in the chairs in front of her desk.

Sophie spoke first. "Sheriff, we just found something out, and it's going to be hard to believe."

The sheriff leaned back in her chair. "That wouldn't be the first time with you, Sophie. Go on."

Sophie began with going to Hilltop and told her what she heard.

Then Jessica picked up the story with going downstairs. "Mr. Jenkins scared us when he said he'd do something to two girls who were also looking for the treasure if they got in his way."

Sheriff Valeska looked startled. "I agree that the situation sounds odd. Who have you talked to about your treasure hunt?"

"Sheriff, we didn't tell anyone that wasn't trustworthy," Sophie said. "You didn't tell anyone I don't know about, right, Jessica?"

"No. We only talked to your parents and Nezzy about it. I don't think any of them would tell another person what we'd said."

The sheriff nodded. "While that all makes sense, how could he have known? Did you make a mistake today and give him that impression?"

"Uh-uh. We said we were interested in seeing the old house. And we *were* interested in it."

Someone coughed and they all turned that direction. Clare Morton said, "Sheriff, I might be the one who said something."

"You!" Sheriff Valeska tapped her fingers on her desk. "Tell me what happened."

"April Sandoval stopped by the other day and mentioned that the girls were searching for the lost Laurence treasure."

Both girls both swung back toward Sheriff Valeska.

"We hadn't talked for a while, and she stopped by to visit. I see that expression on your face, Sophie. Your mother did not come here to tell your secrets. Continue, Clare."

"I passed that nice Mr. Jenkins on the street, and since the treasure ties into Hilltop, I mentioned that two girls were looking for it."

"I see." The sheriff did not look happy. "Why did you do that?"

"He seems so harmless and is always polite and nice. And I thought it was funny." She smiled at them. "I'm sorry, but they're just kids."

"Clare, everything that is said in this office, *everything*, is confidential. You aren't to tell a single person outside of here anything you've overheard. You're new in town, so you don't know that earlier this summer, these two girls foiled a criminal plan and helped us arrest the culprits."

"Really?" She looked from Sophie to Jessica with an expression of disbelief.

The sheriff added, "It would matter to someone that these two were also looking for the treasure."

"Yes, ma'am."

"We'll talk again later, Clare." Turning to Sophie and Jessica, she said, "Here we are again, with me telling you to be careful. I'll check into Jim Jenkins' background and see if something turns up."

Walking away from the sheriff's office, Jessica said, "It's just sinking in that Mr. Jenkins definitely knows that we are searching for the treasure—"

"And that he did mean *us* when he talked about *two girls*."

Jessica shuddered.

"Even I thought this would be a fun little mystery."

"I know. Something to make summer vacation more interesting. We were bored, but . . ." They arrived at Sophie's favorite bench on the sidewalk, the one she always went to when she needed to think.

"The main question is: does this change anything?" Sophie sat down. "Other than us having to keep our eyes open for anything unusual."

Jessica stood beside the bench. "Remember when I said I saw someone wearing black at the cemetery?"

"The crow!" She turned to Jessica. "I'm sorry I doubted you."

"I only caught a flash of black and thought, *Who would care about us checking out a grave?*"

"So you think he's been following us." Sophie started to twist in her seat, then faced forward. "You're standing, so it won't be as obvious. Casually look around us."

Jessica shaded her eyes and checked first down the street, then around in a circle until she could see up the street. "I don't see anything odd. He could be inside a building, watching us, though, and we wouldn't know it."

Sophie stared at the building across the street. "You're right, of course. We need to move into danger mode. We can't assume at any time that we aren't being watched. Well, other than when we're inside a building ourselves. Away from the windows."

"Soph, I wonder if we should tell your parents about what happened today. I can keep it a secret from my parents, since they aren't here and would only worry."

Sophie chewed on her lip. "If we tell my parents, they'll worry too. Remember how they were with the last mystery? Everything turned out fine, but both my parents and yours were a mess."

Jessica said, "Images from that mystery just flashed through my mind. Your parents called my parents. Wow, did they worry. As much as I want to tell them, I guess we should wait until Sheriff Valeska learns for sure who Mr. Jenkins is."

"Yes. Let's wait until we know more."

13

View from Above

When Jessica and Sophie entered Great Finds, Mrs. Sandoval held up two small pieces of paper. "Look what I got! The mayor heard about a carnival that was passing through this area and talked them into coming to Pine Hill for a weekend between locations to do a fund-raiser to save Hilltop. I agreed to donate some of my sales from this weekend to help save the mansion, so the carnival owner gave me and others doing the same thing free passes for the whole family."

She waved the tickets in the air, then frowned and held them close to her chest. "No, you wouldn't like to go to a carnival and go on the rides as many times as you wanted, would you?"

Sophie grabbed at the tickets, but Mrs. Sandoval moved faster and hid them behind her back. "It sounds like fun, Mom."

"Your father and I could meet you at the carnival when I've closed for the day. And we can eat dinner there."

Sophie put her hand on her chest. "Eat fair food? For dinner? Mom, are you okay?"

Mrs. Sandoval laughed. "Just this once. Don't expect us to do this kind of thing very often. And only one dessert."

"I can live with that. How 'bout you, Jessica?"

"Absolutely. I'd like a break from this mystery."

When she heard Sophie gulp, she realized her mistake. What if her aunt asked if they'd learned anything new? She wouldn't lie, and she knew Sophie wouldn't either, but she wasn't sure what her aunt would do if they told her.

Mrs. Sandoval turned and started toward the back of the shop. "I have to put prices on some things that just arrived. You girls can head over to the carnival right now. We'll meet you there about six."

Jessica could hear carnival music as she and Sophie turned down the road to Hilltop. When she could see the mansion, she could also see people swarming over Hilltop's grounds like the hornets around Cody a couple of days ago. There were lines at every ride and all of the food booths.

They gave their tickets at the gate, then wandered around a bit. Sophie stopped in front of the cotton candy booth. "Do you have any money with you?"

"My allowance. I'm not going to buy *that* though." Jessica pointed at the fluffy sweet. She didn't eat sugar straight out of the package, so she didn't see how that could be any good.

"Come on. It's pure sugar. Either pink or blue."

"Maybe I've lived in other countries too long, but that doesn't sound good to me, so unless they come up with a chocolate variety, I don't want to try it."

"Are you saying you've never eaten cotton candy?"

"Uh-huh."

"I need to talk Mom into it. *Everyone* needs to try cotton candy."

They continued on, and Jessica stopped at the deep-fried candy bars.

Sophie held up her hands. "Seriously? After what you said about the dessert I wanted?"

"You're right. But it does sound fun."

"We must both be getting hungry. I hope Mom and Dad get here soon."

After going on three different rides, Jessica felt as if she would forever be spinning and turning from side to side. Holding on to her head, she said, "I need a break from rides."

Sophie slowly turned in a circle. "It's still too early for Mom and Dad. What do you want to do?" She stopped. "Hey, there's Mr. Donadio, Tony's dad. Maybe Tony's here."

Jessica looked that direction. "Where?"

Sophie pointed at a man wearing navy blue pants and a light blue polo shirt.

Jessica felt her face flush as she scanned the area. "Do you see Tony?"

"No. Mr. Donadio is alone right now and seems to be in a hurry."

Jessica looked straight ahead and up. "Let's go on the Ferris wheel."

Sophie grimaced. "After all of the fast-moving rides we've been on, why would you want to go on an old-fashioned Ferris wheel?"

"Ferris wheels are quiet. And they don't move much."

"Exactly."

"I've been flipped from side to side, spun in a circle, and sped downhill screaming enough today. Quiet wins."

"I'd rather flip, spin, or speed again, but I'll go with you."

"And we can't talk about the mystery."

"But—"

"I need a break, Soph. Just peace and quiet."

"Okay. You got it."

The girls showed their tickets, climbed into the seat, and were latched into place.

When the Ferris wheel began its slow circle, Jessica leaned back and felt the stress of the mystery become less and less as they climbed higher and higher. "This is what I needed. And I've never seen Pine Hill from more than a second-story building."

"I think we'll have a good view of the lake from the top." Sophie leaned over the side. "Staring down at all of these people makes me realize that I should never search for clues on the grounds of Hilltop. Too many people have gone back and forth across here over the years. I'm glad we get to have fun here today, but I'm certain we won't find anything to do with the mystery tonight."

When they'd almost reached the top, Jessica pointed to the ground on her side of the Ferris wheel. "There's Mr. Donadio again." She paused for a few seconds. "Oh, no! He's talking to Mr. Jenkins."

"This is a small town, and they know each other, so they must just be *talking*."

"No. Mr. Donadio handed something to Mr. Jenkins, and he handed something back to him. Now they're shaking hands."

Sophie twisted and turned in her seat, obviously hating it that she couldn't see what was happening. When she leaned forward, Jessica grabbed her arm. "Hey, you'll fall out. They're both gone now anyway."

Sophie blew out a breath. "I missed the whole thing!"

Their seat rolled over the top of the wheel and started down the other side.

"Now that I can see below us, there isn't anyone special except my second grade teacher. Miss Becker was nice."

The ride made a few more rotations; then they found themselves stopped at the bottom again, and the attendant was lifting the protective rail so they could get out. As they stepped off the ride, Jessica searched the crowd for Mr. Donadio.

Sophie blew out a deep breath. "I *still* don't see either Mr. Donadio or Mr. Jenkins."

"Sophie, what should we do about what I saw?"

"I don't know, Cousin. It's probably easily explained. I don't want to think Mr. Donadio could be a criminal too."

"Me neither." Jessica scraped her toe on the ground. Suddenly looking up, she said, "What if Mr. Donadio doesn't know about Mr. Jenkins and ends up in danger because we didn't tell him?"

Sophie grimaced. "I hadn't thought of that. I figured he was an adult and could take care of himself. But no one else in this town knows what we know about Mr. Jenkins. They *all* think he's a great guy."

"Soph, we need to find out more. We need to talk to Tony."

"If I didn't know you were a nice person, I'd think you were trying to find a way to bring Tony into another mystery."

"He did help last time."

Sophie sighed. "Yes, he did. I wanted the two of us to solve this one together."

"Maybe next time."

Sophie grinned. "I love that you're into mysteries now."

Jessica held up her hand. "Don't get too happy. I don't think there will be another mystery in this small town in the near future."

"You said that last time."

"I know. I thought we were safe searching for treasure that hundreds of people had searched for."

Sophie checked her watch. "It's almost dinnertime. We're going to have to wait until tomorrow to see

Tony. I don't think we should talk to him about it on the phone."

"Definitely not."

"Let's see if Tony's at the deli in the morning and talk to him outside, where no one can eavesdrop."

"It's a plan." Jessica pointed. "I see your dad now. I'm going to push this out of my mind and have fun tonight."

"Me too. Fair food for dinner? I want to enjoy every bite, because I'll probably be ready to graduate from high school before Mom says we can do that again."

"That's the truth. She loves to eat healthy."

They hurried up to Mr. Sandoval.

"Sophie, your mother has a surprise," he said. "Come on, both of you."

As they turned to follow him, Jessica could hear loud voices from the other side of the carnival, growing louder with every step they took. When they could see the source of the shouting, they found a woman on a seat overhanging a water-filled dunk tank. People threw balls at a target on the side of the tank, hoping to hit it and drop her into the water.

As they neared it, Sophie shook her head. "I wouldn't want to be that woman."

"Your mother surprised me when she agreed to hop up there."

Sophie pointed. "That's Mom?"

Mr. Sandoval nodded.

Jessica giggled. "At least she didn't ask *you* to do it."

They watched for a few minutes. Then Mr.

Sandoval got a sneaky smile on his face that reminded Jessica of his daughter. He left for a few minutes and returned with a basketful of balls.

"Do you girls want to give it a shot?"

Sophie spun around and stared at her dad. Then she got that same smile. "Yes, I do." She picked up three of the balls and stood in line.

Jessica pictured her aunt falling in the water because of a ball she'd thrown. "I think I'm going to pass on this."

Mr. Sandoval said, "Go ahead, Jessica. April won't be angry. She did it to support Hilltop."

"If you're sure . . ."

He nodded.

"Okay." Balls in hand, Jessica waited behind Sophie. "I doubt I'll hit anything."

Sophie turned toward Jessica, her dark brown eyes sparkling. "I was on the softball team when I was little. I'll hit it."

When her turn came up, Sophie stepped forward and her mother cried out, "Oh, no!"

Sophie took aim and threw the ball. A bang signaled the ball hitting the target, and a splash told the rest of the story. Jessica handed the balls back to her uncle. "I think one person in the family knocking her down is enough."

He gave the balls to some people watching off to the side. "You may be right. Let's get something to eat."

14

Guilty Dad?

When Jessica and Sophie found a list of chores posted on the refrigerator the next morning, Sophie groaned. "At least there isn't any housecleaning involved. We don't have any clues to chase this morning, and the deli won't open until 11:00 a.m, so helping Mom is no biggie."

She read through the list again. "This is Dad's handwriting, so Mom must have called him. She wants us to bring paper towels from home to her shop and to mail some things at the post office. We can do all of that this morning."

Sophie carried the three-pack of paper towels under one arm. When they were about a block from Great Finds, Sheriff Valeska drove by in a sheriff's car. She pulled over to the curb, and as they were passing by, rolled down the window. "Are you girls being careful?"

"As careful as we can be when we're not sure what we're being careful of."

The sheriff blinked, then nodded. "It's surprising to me, but I actually understood what you meant." She motioned them closer.

Sophie leaned in the car window and asked in a low voice, "Any news on Mr. Jenkins?"

"Nothing."

Sophie stood so quickly she bonked her head on the window frame. She rubbed the spot and winced. "How is that possible?"

"When I say 'nothing,' I mean absolutely nothing. It's as though he didn't exist until he started working for Harold Laurence."

Jessica leaned next to her, "What does that mean?"

Sophie pointed to her chest. "I know. He isn't who he says he is, right?"

"Most likely. I don't know any more yet. I hope to soon. In the meantime—"

Sophie interrupted. "Be careful."

"Yes. We don't know who he really is. He might be a nice man who just changed his name because he didn't like it. But he might also have a criminal reason for his name change."

As they watched Sheriff Valeska drive off, Sophie said, "Let's hurry up so we can get to the deli."

"I hope your mom doesn't ask us to work and make it so we can't get to the deli."

"I agree. We *need* to talk to Tony, but I don't want to tell her—or anyone else—about what we saw until we know more. It wouldn't be right for people to think badly about Mr. Donadio if he's innocent."

Mrs. Sandoval was busy with a customer when they got back to the shop. They put the supplies away in the back, picked up the mail where she said she'd put it, along with the cash needed to pay for the postage, and hurried back out. Sophie gave a little wave to her mother as she opened the door to leave.

Mrs. Sandoval called out, "Come back here this afternoon. I have a couple of projects for the two of you to work on."

"We weren't fast enough," Sophie said to Jessica as the door closed behind them.

"You could never be fast enough to get out of work with your mom."

Sophie shrugged. "True."

Once they'd reached the post office, they waited in line, mailed Mrs. Sandoval's things, then hurried over to Donadio's Deli. Every time Jessica pictured them talking to Tony, it didn't go well. "Sophie, it might stand out less to everyone else if we eat lunch and try to talk to Tony quietly there."

"You're probably right. It's a good thing we *did* save our allowance."

Tony placed the Open sign in the window as they arrived. Eating earlier than normal, they had the deli to themselves. As the glass door closed behind them, Sophie whispered, "Remember: the fact that we're searching for the treasure and all of the clues we've found are secrets. We're only here to ask in a sneaky way about Tony's dad so we can take him off the list of suspects. Since everyone thinks Mr. Jenkins is super nice, we'd better only tell Tony about him if we absolutely have to."

Jessica could keep a secret with the best of them. "Yes. We'll be subtle. I won't tell any secrets." Scenes of their last mystery flashed through her mind. Jessica had spilled the secret to Tony then. Heat climbed up her neck, which she knew made her face red. "I really *can* keep a secret."

"I hope so."

"I know I didn't keep the secret last time, but I will this time."

As they ordered their food from Tony, Jessica felt melty inside.

Tony smirked as he set their food on the table minutes later. "Hot on the trail of any criminals?" He walked over to the counter and picked up a spray bottle and rag, then sprayed the table beside them and started wiping it off.

Jessica leaned forward. "T-r-e-a-s-u-r-e," she said slowly.

Sophie stared at her cousin. "Jessica!"

"I opened my big mouth again, didn't I?" The secret spiller had struck again.

Tony stopped what he was doing and eyed them suspiciously. "Actual treasure?"

Sophie said, "Sort of." She wavered her hand. "Yes, but no."

"Yes, you found treasure or yes, you're searching for treasure?"

Jessica excitedly added, "We're hunting treasure."

She did a happy dance in her seat. "I love how those words sound. Jessica Ballow, treasure hunter."

Tony threw down the rag and sat in a chair at their table. "With pretty much anyone else, I'd say, no way, you won't actually find treasure. But you guys have a track record."

Sophie said, "The 'yes, but no' is that it's the Laurence treasure."

He pushed back his chair. "Not only have I looked for it, but my parents, grandparents, and great-grandparents all looked for that treasure. They didn't find anything, and as far as I know, no one ever has."

Jessica said, "Yes, but we know things no one else in town knows."

Sophie poked her cousin's arm. "Jessica!"

Jessica sheepishly said, "I'm sorry."

Tony leaned forward. "What?"

Jessica stared at Sophie. Then Sophie said, "Okay. Tony helped us last time."

"Give." He motioned forward with his hand.

Sophie glanced over at the door when it chimed, announcing a group of four people entering the restaurant. "I think we should talk to you outside, Tony."

The girls got up and went outside. Tony joined them a few minutes later.

Jessica took a deep breath to calm her nerves and asked him, "How well do you know Mr. Jenkins?"

"How well?" Tony shrugged. "He's a customer. He lives in Pine Hill."

Sophie scanned the street, probably to make sure no one could overhear her, but leaned closer to Tony anyway. "Mr. Jenkins hasn't been to your house for dinner? Your dad doesn't play golf or bowl with him or anything like that?"

Tony scrunched up his face. "No. Why are you asking me that? Hey, you aren't investigating my dad, are you?" His face quickly turned stormy.

Jessica touched his arm. "We don't want to. It's just that we saw your dad at the carnival last night." She didn't add that she'd seen him with a criminal.

"So what? Most of the town was there." He crossed his arms over his chest and glared at them.

This wasn't going well.

"Sophie, let's just tell him."

"Tell me what?" he said.

"We saw your dad with Mr. Jenkins, and it looked like they were doing business together." When Tony seemed confused, Jessica added, "Mr. Jenkins is not who you think he is."

Tony raised his hands. "This is about Mr. Jenkins? He's a nice guy. What are you talking about?" He stepped toward the door of the deli. "I need to get back to work."

"We overheard Mr. Jenkins talking to another man. There's no question that they're both criminals, and Mr. Jenkins is conning the town."

"That's ridiculous. He took good care of Mr. Laurence and everything in the house."

"Tony, he has many of the house's treasures in his

room in the basement, treasures that everyone believes were sold to help Mr. Laurence."

He leaned against the window. "He couldn't. I know for a fact that Mrs. Bowman's sister cleans Hilltop. She would have seen that and told her sister, and you know Mrs. Bowman can't keep a secret."

"Mr. Jenkins does her a favor by not having her clean his room."

"Wow. It's hard to believe." He suddenly stood up straight and his eyes narrowed. "But you asked about my father."

Jessica explained what she'd seen.

Someone else walked past them and into the deli. "I have to get back to work," Tony repeated. "When I see my dad, I'll tell him you saw him at the carnival and see if he explains why." He opened the door to the deli. "And if I can, I'll come over tonight, and you can tell me what other clues you have."

As the door closed behind him, Jessica blew out her breath. "I wasn't sure about that for a minute."

"Me neither. I didn't think enough about this to realize we were accusing Mr. Donadio of being a criminal. That was stupid."

"Yes, it was. We might have lost a friend for our carelessness. I hope Tony has good news for us tonight."

Just then, Nezzy's housekeeper, Amanda Easton, walked by the deli. She carried a bag with the town's craft store's name written across it in bold red letters. When she noticed them, she stopped. "I'm glad to see you girls. Walk with me while I go to the candy store. Nezzy loves their cherry-filled chocolates."

She raced down the sidewalk, and they hurried to catch up with her.

Sophie said, "It must be fun to work for Nezzy."

"Oh, my, yes. She's delightful, but a little demanding." Miss Easton smiled to soften the comment. "I just bought her a new book for her memories. This will be her second one this year, her B. She asked me to invite you over to go through her many memory books, if you'd like to."

Jessica pictured being bored for hours reading through an old lady's memories.

Sophie gave a polite, but not-quite-real smile. "Please thank her for the offer."

Jessica said, "I've never heard of memory books. That must be something you do around here."

Miss Easton stopped. Laughing, she said, "Of course you'd say no to something with that name. They're scrapbooks filled with things from Nezzy's life. Mr. Laurence was her friend, so many of the memories have to do with him."

Sophie felt her heart race. They'd figured the newspaper wouldn't have much to help them, but they might finally get some answers from the scrapbooks. "Can we come over tomorrow afternoon?"

Miss Easton smiled at them. "Certainly. I'll expect you at two." She waved as she hurried away, turning the corner onto Dogwood where Sophie knew the candy store sat.

"Jessica, we'd better get over to Great Finds. Let's hope that the work we have to do is something we don't mind."

"I just hope I don't have to dust. I've learned that there's a lot to dust in a shop filled with antiques."

When they got to Great Finds, they discovered that they were to unpack some new items. Mrs. Sandoval directed Jessica to one cluster of boxes, and Sophie to another. Each item was to be carefully unwrapped. Then Mrs. Sandoval would price the item and set it in its proper place for sale.

Jessica peeled bubble wrap from around a large, green-and-yellow vase. "I love doing this. It's a little like Christmas."

Mrs. Sandoval said, "I feel that way too, even though I saw everything when I bought it. We have one more box to do, and then we can all go home to dinner."

After dinner, Sophie offered to do the dishes and said Jessica would help. When they were alone in the kitchen, Sophie explained, "I did this for a reason. I thought we could talk about what we'll do if Tony's dad turns out to be one of the gang." Sophie rinsed dishes and handed them to Jessica to load into the dishwasher.

"Now that I've had time to think about it, I doubt that's what we'll discover. Mr. Donadio isn't someone who just came to town. He's lived here a long time."

"As long as I remember."

"Let's assume he's okay." Jessica tucked a pot into the corner of the bottom rack. "I hope that's all the dishes, because this is almost full."

"That's it." Sophie added, "The more I think about asking Tony about his dad, the more I realize that we might have started something ugly. Let's wait on the front porch so we can talk to Tony alone when he gets here."

Jessica blew out a big breath. "Good idea. If there is a problem, maybe we can talk to him quietly before we have to tell anyone else."

"Like the sheriff."

"Yes, like the sheriff. I still have the photo and keys in my purse. I'll get it so we can show them to Tony."

They sat on the porch, Jessica on a rocker and Sophie on the porch swing. A car pulled into the driveway at about seven o'clock. Tony stepped out of the car, closed the door, and waved as his dad backed out and drove away. Then he walked toward the girls, carrying a bulging bag that he held up when he got closer.

"Ice cream and toppings. We can make sundaes."

"Chocolate?" Jessica asked.

"Of course. I wouldn't forget the hot fudge sauce for you. Or the strawberry sauce for Sophie. And I have whipped cream and nuts."

Sophie and Jessica looked at each other. Did this mean everything was okay? Which one of them should ask? Jessica pointed at Sophie.

"Is everything all right at home, Tony?"

"Very subtle. I did what I said and told my dad that you'd seen him at the carnival. He got upset."

Sophie stood up. "I'm sorry, Tony."

"No, not because he was guilty of something." He motioned for her to sit back down. "Because he was handing Mr. Jenkins a bill for a dinner the deli catered at Hilltop for Mr. Jenkins and some of his friends."

Jessica beat her to asking, "Why would that upset him?"

"He'd mailed the bill to Mr. Jenkins six months ago and again two months ago, but it hadn't been paid. Mr. Jenkins said it never arrived, so Dad told him he'd personally bring it to him at Hilltop. Except when he got there—"

"There was a carnival." Sophie did sit down now, feeling more relieved than she thought she would at learning that Mr. Donadio wasn't guilty.

"Dad had to track him down at the carnival. You saw him handing Mr. Jenkins the bill and Mr. Jenkins handing Dad a check for the amount." He lifted up the bag again. "Are you ready for dessert?"

"Always," Jessica held open the door for him and he carried it through to the kitchen.

Inside, Sophie explained to her parents that Tony had brought dessert. Her mother didn't want a sundae, but her dad asked for one with hot fudge. Sophie made his, brought it to him, and fixed her own after Tony and Jessica.

The three of them took their sundaes onto the front porch—Sophie returning to the porch swing,

Jessica and Tony each taking a rocking chair. All three dove into their frosty desserts.

When they were about halfway done, Tony asked, "Do you have any actual clues to the treasure?"

Jessica held up her purse and stared at Sophie, who nodded once. Jessica pulled out the photo and two keys. She started the story of how they'd found each, with Sophie jumping in to add things Jessica'd missed.

Tony took the photo of the house from Jessica, turning it over to check the blank back. "It just says 'Hilltop.' He handed it back. "I know the story of the gold in the moonlight. I don't see anything that seems like a clue. Who knows what that second key fits?"

Sophie hated to admit it, but Tony was right. How would these help them find treasure?

"These things must be clues," Jessica said, laying the keys and photo on the arm of her rocking chair. "Two of them were hidden in secret compartments in Harold Laurence's desk."

"That makes them more interesting, but I still only see a photo and two keys, one that's already been used for its purpose. The photo says, 'Hilltop.' That isn't very helpful."

Tony stared into his ice cream. "Nezzy Grant told you the desk was important?"

Jessica dipped her spoon into the fudge sauce. "Uh-huh. I know it looks like an old photo and keys, but who would hide unimportant things that well?"

Sophie held her spoon in the air. "Especially the second key, the larger one. That took a while to find."

Tony reached over and picked up that key, turning it over in his hand. "I admit this *key* could *unlock* the secret of the lost treasure . . ." His voice trailed off and he grinned, obviously waiting for comments.

Jessica groaned. "I can't believe you said that."

Sophie snickered. "I can't believe I didn't say it."

Laughing, Tony added, "When you consider the number of doors and other things with keyholes in Pine Hill, this could take a long time."

Jessica scraped the last bite of hot fudge from her bowl. "We could never try them all."

Sophie set down her empty bowl and reached for the photo. "Wouldn't Mr. Laurence want someone to find the treasure? Otherwise, why leave the key in the desk?"

Continuing, Sophie said, "I just thought of something: what if Mr. Laurence wasn't the man in the woods that the doctor saw that night? It was dark, and the doctor was in a hurry."

Jessica tapped her fingers on her cheek. "I see how you're thinking. Or what if it was him, but it wasn't really a bag of gold? Maybe it was a bag of nails to build his house, or something else that could shine in the moonlight."

Sophie added. "Or a stranger who was about the same size as Mr. Laurence and had his hair cut similarly who did have gold, but he put it on a wagon and drove away with it that night?"

Jessica said, "Oh my, Soph, that is good."

Tony added, "Or we may be missing something. Go

•111•

over everything one more time. I have to work tomorrow, my family is doing something that night, and Sunday we're taking inventory at the deli. I can't help either day."

Jessica said, "Did we tell you that Mr. Jenkins asked about us at Bananas?"

Tony stopped with his spoon halfway to his mouth. "Let me get this straight. You just told me that Mr. Jenkins knows you're looking for the treasure because Clare at the sheriff's office goofed?"

Sophie said, "Right. But he hasn't bothered us."

"He asked about you two at Bananas. He told Lester about two girls. And you're certain that Mr. Jenkins isn't a nice man."

A clatter sounded when Sophie and Jessica both dropped their spoons.

Jessica reached to pick hers up from the porch floor. "I don't like hearing all of those things combined."

"Sophie and Jessica, you'd better be careful and keep looking over your shoulders."

Tony's dad pulled into the driveway a short time later, and they watched him drive away with Tony. Even with what their friend had said, Jessica knew the treasure was out there and *they* would be the ones to find it. She also knew they had to be very careful.

15

Cleaning for Clues

Sophie wasn't sure she'd fall sleep with all of the clues running through her head, but she'd dropped right off. Probably because she was so tired.

Stretching in bed the next morning, Sophie could see Jessica moving around like she was awake. "Let's grab something for breakfast in town this morning and get right on the mystery. We didn't come up with anything new last night."

Neither she nor Jessica had mentioned the key mark on her arm to Tony the night before. She felt a little guilty about that, but she wanted to see if the two of them found anything first. Besides, he had to work and wouldn't be happy about not being in on the search.

Jessica grabbed her robe, but didn't say a word as she headed for the bathroom. She must realize she woke up grouchy. Mornings hadn't always gone well before they'd come up with the system of having her head straight for the shower without conversation.

When the door closed and the shower turned on, Sophie said, "Whew! I'm glad we figured this out." She picked up a book to read as she waited for Jessica.

"Much better," Jessica said a short time later when she stepped out of the bathroom, rubbing her hair with a towel. "I thought anything I tried to say this morning would come out grumpy."

"It amazes me that someone as smart as you can't work around that." Sophie climbed out of bed, headed into the bathroom for her shower and came back afterward feeling ready to take on the day. She found her cousin putting on makeup.

Jessica set her mascara down on the dresser. "I didn't fall asleep for a while last night. I think chocolate is a good idea this morning."

"Chocolate for breakfast? Where? And can I get something without chocolate there?"

"A chocolate chocolate-chip muffin from Bananas would work."

An image of one of Mrs. Bowman's awesome banana-blueberry muffins popped into her mind. "Deal."

"Let me get my sneakers and jeans on."

When Jessica was ready, she searched for Sophie and found her dressed and on the front porch. The cousins walked down the porch steps, but then Sophie paused. "Shortcut through the woods or beside the road?"

Jessica stepped beside her. "I never thought I'd

have to pick one over the other because of bad guys again." She looked to her right toward the woods, then down the driveway to the road. "Road. I think we'd better be careful."

"Yes. We haven't seen anyone dangerous yet—"

"Hold it. Mr. Jenkins and Lenny were creepy and sounded dangerous to me."

"I guess I was trying to see them as fellow treasure hunters."

"Who just happened to sound scary when they talked about us?"

"I see your point. The road wins."

As they walked beside the road, Jessica said, "We need to check out the inside of Hilltop. *Really* check it out. And we have to see if the brick with the key on it is part of the mystery."

"I know. The mansion has to be the answer to everything. We didn't have a chance to search for clues inside the house." Sophie snapped her fingers. "I remember that Miss Walker works at the mansion on Thursday and—"

"Saturday," Jessica said. "I'm fairly certain Mrs. Bowman said that. Since she was at the mansion two days ago . . ."

Sophie pumped air with her fist. "Yes! She must be there today. Maybe we can look around inside when Mr. Jenkins is at lunch."

"He could come back any second. And how would we explain being there again? I lay in bed last night trying to come up with a way around Mr. Jenkins. I don't want to try to search again when he's there. And he isn't only there sometimes. He lives in the mansion, so he's almost always there."

They walked without speaking. Jessica was trying to come up with a plan and figured Sophie was too.

After a bit, Sophie said, "Maybe we'll get a break in the case and Mr. Jenkins will go to the city for the day. Or fishing. Or something else."

"Those things only help a little, because Miss Walker will probably tell him we were there when he arrives home later today, and it will stand out if we were the only unexpected visitors."

The girls opened the door to Bananas—and froze. The man they'd been talking about stood at the front counter, handing Mrs. Bowman cash. With his usual smile on his face, he said to her, "I'm sure these muffins will be delicious as always."

Mrs. Bowman blushed. "You'll have some home-made muffins for your drive and the first couple days of your vacation. Make sure you eat a good breakfast the rest of the week."

"Nothing will be as wonderful as what you make." He picked up a yellow box and turned to leave. When he spotted them, he said, "I hope you girls didn't get drenched in the storm two days ago."

Thinking quickly of something honest to say, Jessica politely answered, "No, sir. We ran down the road when we left."

Mrs. Bowman put her hand on her cheek and sighed when he went out the door. "What a *nice* man."

Jessica could tell that Sophie was having to grit her teeth to not tell her the opposite. "Is he going on vacation to a beach or somewhere beautiful like that?" Jessica watched him climb into a car parked at the curb and drive off. This could be their chance.

"He never says. Mr. Jenkins is here almost every day when he's in town, but he's gone about a week most months. He always brightens my morning when he comes in."

Sophie and Jessica quickly bought a muffin each, Jessica's filled with chocolate and Sophie's fruity, ordering them to go instead of choosing to sit at one of the small tables Mrs. Bowman had recently added.

Outside, Jessica said, "I'm so glad we heard that."

"Mr. Jenkins will be gone from Hilltop for days." Sophie stood in front of Bananas with the bag of muffins clutched in her hand.

"Soph, are we going to eat our muffins?"

Sophie held out the bag as if she were in a trance.

"Hello? Sophie?"

"Huh?" She blinked at Jessica. "Oh, sorry. I've been trying to figure out a way for us to get back inside Hilltop, but have it seem natural, not like we're on a treasure hunt. It's city property, so it's legal for us to be there, but I don't think we should ask for another tour."

An idea popped into Jessica's mind. She tugged on Sophie's sleeve and pulled her over to a bench on the sidewalk. "Sit. Eat. I have an idea."

An hour later, they were knocking on Hilltop's

kitchen door. When Miss Walker answered, Sophie spoke. "We noticed when we visited before that there was more work here than you had time for. Jessica and I would like to help."

Jessica held up a bucket filled with cleaning supplies, all borrowed from Great Finds. "The room at the front of the house is so pretty that we wanted to make it shiny and clean."

The older woman smiled and ushered them inside. "That's kind of you two. As much as I hate to admit it, I can't do much more than clean the same rooms each week in the two days I give to the city. I have too many other things going on in my life to take on the rest of the house."

Miss Walker walked them into the connected room. "Now that they've voted to tear it down, there probably isn't a point, but I'd like to see it clean one more time. If you girls need me, I'll be upstairs. I'm working on a project in one of the bedrooms."

The girls pulled out their cleaning supplies as Miss Walker left. When she disappeared up the stairs, Sophie said, "I wish your idea hadn't included us cleaning."

"I hope it's worth it."

Sophie pulled on rubber gloves, opened a trash bag, and started filling it with garbage. "Let's clean as quickly as we can so we'll have time to check things out. I want to make sure we have lots of detective time while we're here."

Jessica glanced around the room and started for the

door. "There's icky stuff in piles on this side of the room's floor." She left the room, returning minutes later with a broom. While sweeping, she said, "You know, Sophie, Mr. Jenkins has lived here for years. He must have checked everywhere for the treasure."

Sophie set aside the bag of trash and picked up paper towels and window cleaner. She sprayed a window, then wiped it dry. "I know Mr. Jenkins did everything he could think of, but he didn't have the clues from the desk." Sophie stepped back to see her work, nodded approval, and moved on to the next window.

"Uh, Soph?"

"Yes?" Sophie turned around to find Jessica staring at the floor. "The animal that got inside left these little brown pellets behind, didn't he?"

Sophie laughed. "Yes, he—or she—did. And you definitely want to wear gloves if you get anywhere near those pellets."

"I thought so. It's poop." Jessica put her gloves on and wiped the messy part off the floor, then carefully dropped the paper towel into the trash bag. "Yuck. I can't believe I'm actually doing this. It's even harder for me to believe that I'm doing this so I can help solve a mystery."

When they'd almost finished, Sophie stepped back and looked around. "This must have been a fancy room when it was new."

"I know." Jessica dropped a final paper towel into the bag. "I'll dust and you get the mop."

A half hour later, Sophie said, "Gorgeous. We finished quickly."

"It's pretty now. Let's hurry downstairs and see if that brick is important. After that, we can go through the rest of the house. I hope Miss Walker is too busy to check our progress."

"Me too. She thinks Mr. Jenkins is wonderful and would tell him about our treasure hunting."

They hurried to the kitchen and down the stairs. Sophie pulled out a small flashlight she'd tucked in her back pocket and pointed it at the corner.

Jessica knelt and ran her hand over bricks until she found the rough one. "This is it!"

Sophie knelt beside her and pushed on the sides of the brick. "I think this is loose. I need something to pry it out with."

Jessica stood and ran around the room. "I finally found a screwdriver on a workbench in the corner." She moved beside Sophie and put the blade of the screwdriver into the area beside the brick, working it loose. When it was about to fall, Sophie caught it.

Jessica said, "Nice save. That might have made a crash that would be heard throughout the house." Sophie shone the light into the hole left by the brick, and Jessica tried to see inside. "There's a white thing in here." Jessica reached into the hole and brought out a wooden box that wasn't much larger than the photo they'd found.

Sophie shone the light on it. "This box has a key painted on it."

"Mr. Laurence sure liked keys." Jessica lifted the lid and Sophie leaned over to see. "A piece of paper is inside. It's yellowed, so he must have put it here a very long time ago."

"37B is written on it. Nothing more. What could that mean?" Sophie picked up the brick and slid it back in place. "We'd better get out of here. I don't want Miss Walker to tell Mr. Jenkins we were down here. He'd wonder why."

Back upstairs, they returned to the room Mr. Jenkins had left them in while he was in his office. Sophie said, "We can spend more time on the box when we leave here. Let's search the mansion while we have the chance."

Jessica wandered through the parlor, now dining room. "What are we looking for? Do you have any idea? Or is this another of those 'we'll know it when we see it' times?"

"To answer your questions: I don't know. I don't. And yes."

Jessica laughed.

They went from room to room. "Whatever we're looking for wouldn't be obvious. It has to be a place that wouldn't have occurred to Mr. Jenkins."

Sophie paused at the stairway and gazed up.

Jessica said, "I don't think we can explain why we're upstairs. Unless you want to clean more."

Sophie shook her head. "Considering the holes in the roof, I have a feeling that the upstairs is much worse than the main floor."

Jessica brushed her hands on her pants. "I've had enough of this place. Dirt and things I never, ever wanted to get close to are all around me. And on me. I don't think there are any clues here." She sat on the bottom step, feeling discouraged.

"I'm surprised, but I agree with you."

"Really?" Jessica brightened up. "I thought you'd tell me we had to keep at it, that we'd find the clue if we tried harder."

Sophie sat beside her. "I'm starting to think you're right about what you said earlier. If there was a clue in here, if the treasure was in the mansion, Mr. Jenkins would have found it earlier. He didn't find the brick, probably because it was in a dark corner of the basement, but I bet he's been through every inch of the rest of the house." She stood. "Let's go home."

"Oh, thank you! We said we'd go to Nezzy's this afternoon, and I want to get that done so I can take a shower to wash all of this grime off me." Jessica stood.

They shouted a good-bye to Miss Walker and grabbed their bucket of cleaning supplies.

Walking toward the door, Jessica said, "Sophie, something just occurred to me. I've thought of finding the treasure as another mystery, something we need to solve."

"It is. What's your point?"

"This may be a mystery, but it's also a lot of money—if what the story says is true. What are we going to do with all that money if we find it?"

Sophie brushed off the front of her shirt with her

hand. "If it's in Hilltop or anywhere on the property, the treasure belongs to the city."

"True. What if it isn't?" What if it's somewhere that no one owns, and we can keep it?"

"I see pictures of things I could buy flashing in front of me." Sophie grabbed for the doorknob, holding on tight. "Whew. Thinking about this makes me light-headed."

"Me too. We'd be rich."

Sophie chuckled. "What am I thinking? It wouldn't matter, because our parents would decide what we do with it. They'd be happy if we paid for college."

"Maybe we could do something great with it, perhaps help people."

"I hope we get the chance to figure it out."

Jessica said, "We'd better hurry. We need to get to Nezzy's by two."

"I keep thinking, where else could the treasure be hidden, Jessica? It must be here."

"I wonder if the clue we just found is sending us to a new place. But what's a 37B?"

Sophie patted the pocket of her backpack, which held the box. "Let's make a list of everything that could have a 37B."

"I think that will be a short list. If we decide it might be at Hilltop, we can come back next week—if Mr. Jenkins hasn't returned."

"We need to walk faster to get to Nezzy's on time. Let's think about the next step in solving our mystery on the way."

Jessica held up her hand to hide a smile. Sophie could sound so mysterious. Then she stopped smiling. Last time they'd gotten involved in a mystery, it had gotten more than a little dangerous. Maybe she shouldn't be smiling too much.

16

The Memory Room

Climbing the steep stairs to Nezzy's house, Jessica said, "We can spend an hour or less here and still have time to do some other sleuthing today. I don't see how it could take very long to flip through a few old scrapbooks."

When they rang the bell, Miss Easton opened the door and ushered them inside. "Nezzy is resting. I'm to take you to her memory room."

Sophie and Jessica followed the older woman. The housekeeper led them down a hall and stopped at double doors. She reached for handles on the doors and pushed the doors to the side into pockets in the wall. An antique-looking orange-and-gold sofa straight ahead caught Jessica's attention when she stepped into the room. Her Aunt April would probably like it. It wasn't until Sophie gasped that she turned her gaze upward.

Sophie's voice shook a little when she said, "They're filled with books." She cleared her throat.

"The shelves are filled with what must be hundreds of scrapbooks."

"Three hundred and thirty, to be exact," Miss Easton said. "There will be three hundred and thirty-one when Nezzy finishes the book she's working on now."

Jessica gulped. They'd be here longer than an hour. A lot longer than that if they needed to go through every one of these books.

Sophie said, "Nezzy knew Mr. Laurence most of her life, so he could be in almost all of them."

"Quite true. Each is labeled by year." Miss Easton pointed at the spine of the newest book. "I'll leave you girls with your project. If you need anything, pull that cord and I'll come." She pointed at a heavy gold cord hanging next to the sofa.

When she'd left, Jessica asked, "Which 165 books do *you* want to do?" She giggled.

Sophie stared up at the shelves. "This is a *giant* job. Maybe we should start at the beginning." She crossed the room. Running her finger along the edge of the shelf, she said, "Nezzy's a great record keeper. They're not only labeled by year, but she also has an A, B, C, etc., for the order of them in the year." She pulled four of the scrapbooks off the shelf and handed two to Jessica, who carried hers to a round table in the middle of the room. Sophie sat down on the sofa with her two.

Jessica carefully opened the old book and gently turned the pages. It was filled with photos and other pieces of memories, like a dried flower or a ticket from an event, each held in the book by the little black corners they were tucked into. A strip of paper with a description typed on it was glued under each item.

When she reached the end of the first book, Jessica pushed it aside and opened the next one. "You know, Sophie, this really is searching for a needle in a haystack, as our grandfather likes to say."

"I know. I'm trying to stay positive. We're not only searching through hundreds of books, but we don't have even a small idea of what we're looking for. We're just hoping there's a great clue somewhere in all of this." Sophie waved her hand toward the full bookshelves.

Jessica watched Sophie finish one book and open her second.

"Jessica, hold it. What if—" She stood and went over to the bookshelves, following them along the wall again.

"Soph, what are you doing?"

"37B."

Jessica whispered, "Just like in the box." As she stood, her chair fell backward, but she caught it just before it crashed to the wood floor. Righting the chair, she said, "Bring it over here" and pushed her two books to the side.

Sophie did and set it down. Then she flipped through the pages one by one. About halfway through, one page landed harder than the others. "This page seems different."

Jessica leaned in closer. "Different how?" She lifted it up. "Sophie—"

"What?"

"It's thicker at the top."

Sophie flipped the page back and forth. "You're right."

"The typed words under it say, 'Harold and I in front of the new stained glass windows he bought for the church.' This must be a clue he wanted someone to find."

"I agree."

Sophie laid the book flat in front of her and slipped one corner out of the black piece that held it.

"Careful."

When she'd taken it out of the second black corner, Sophie lifted the photo up and tilted the photo album. A tiny envelope fell out.

Jessica picked it up. "Someone wrote, 'My dear Nezzy Grant' on this. I think it's the same handwriting as the envelope with the key."

Sophie stared over her shoulder at the closed door. "I, um, wonder, um, if we should open it."

"Sophie!"

"Okay. You're right. Let's find out if Mrs. Grant can see us now." She pulled the cord, and it wasn't long before Miss Easton opened the door to the room.

When they told her what they'd found and showed her the envelope, she smiled widely. "Let me take this upstairs. I think Nezzy will want to see you." She left with the memory book and envelope.

While they waited, they flipped through the rest of the book.

Jessica said, "Other than learning about things that happened in 1937, I don't see anything else that seems to be a clue."

"Me neither."

Miss Easton returned and gestured them over. "Nezzy's very excited. Follow me."

Nezzy's over-the-top decorating style continued at the top of the stairs. What must have been family portraits going back hundreds of years, all in big gold or silver-colored frames, lined the purple-painted hallway.

Jessica said, "I feel like I'm in a castle in England. They often have many old pictures like this. Of course, not with a purple wall."

Miss Easton said, "These aren't Nezzy's relatives. She visited a castle and wanted her home to be like the castle."

Sophie and Jessica grinned at each other, and Jessica wondered whose relatives these were.

When they entered Nezzy's room, they found her propped up in bed. The walls of the room were covered with framed pictures of what must be her actual family and friends, since they were mostly black-and-white photos. From the way people were dressed in them, some must have been taken about the same time as the photo in the 37B book.

"Sit, girls, sit." The old lady pointed at two chairs Miss Easton must have brought over, since they were beside the bed. "It seems my dear friend left me one last note." She held up the envelope and the piece of paper that had been folded up inside it. "The message is actually for you two."

"Us?" Sophie pointed at herself, then Jessica.

Nezzy nodded. "He left other clues, and someone had to be clever enough to figure out those clues and come here. I didn't mention this before, but Herbert loved mysteries whether it was a book or a movie."

"Me too!" Sophie said.

Jessica added, "She does *love* a mystery. That's how we end up in the middle of these things."

Sophie leaned forward. "Is there a clue in the letter?"

"No."

"No! Are you sure?"

Nezzy cackled. "I'm sure. The treasure's story is in this letter. There *is* a treasure."

Sophie leaned back and fanned her face with her hand. "Wow. A real treasure. I hoped . . ."

"You girls are the first to get this close. Herbert wrote:

"My dear Nezzy,

If you are reading this, you or someone else has most likely found the photo in the desk and the hidden box."

Nezzy looked up at them.

Sophie answered. "Yes. We just found the box."

She nodded and continued:

"*Those clues have brought them to you. Tell them to study the photo and the caption. It will lead them to the treasure. I also want the story of the gold to be out in the open now.*

"*When my father was young, he rode on horseback with a group of four friends in the Wild West. One day, one of them pointed at a wagon train in the distance and commented that it was probably coming from a mine. Another one said they should rob it and be set for life. All agreed to the plan, except my father. He tried to talk them out of it and rode along, hoping to find a way to stop them. But he didn't and they robbed the train, which did have gold from a mine, but in a crazy twist, the gold was under the control of other robbers.*

"*Those men shouted that they'd hauled that gold a long way and it was theirs. They had a shootout. My father jumped onto the wagon and drove it off so the shooting would stop. The men with my father all trusted him, so when they caught up with him, they asked him to take it to a town, put it in boxes, and ship it home. He did box it up, but shipped it another direction, hoping to be able to return it to the mine later. He never could figure out which mine it had come from.*

"*My father moved here, took a new name, and hid the gold. I melted it down and hid it.*"

Sophie stood. "What a story!"

"Yes. Herbert was a good man. He has one more sentence about the treasure: '*I made sure the gold belongs to Pine Hill.*'"

Jessica stared at Sophie. "That must mean that it's on land that belongs to the city of Pine Hill."

Nezzy said, "Yes. He left his land and home to the city. He added for me: '*And my dear Nezzy, I made my money investing in oil. I never told you that because you love a mystery almost as much as I do.*'" She gave a big grin. "Another mystery solved."

She stared at the open memory book lying beside her in the bed. "Isn't he handsome in this picture? Harold was a perfectionist and meticulous when he was younger. Everything had to be just so."

The girls looked at each other and Jessica shrugged. This didn't sound like useful information, but they'd be nice to her. "Yes, ma'am. You mean how he dressed?"

"Everything. When he paid for the church to be built, the builder didn't put the right stained glass window in the right window hole in the church. He had them remove all five of them and install them again as he requested. And I remember way back, before his early cabin burned down, that he rebuilt the old well there. He said it wasn't in good shape. I said, 'Who cares? You don't live there anymore.' He just nodded and did it anyway."

Sophie said, "We found what was left of a cabin in the woods. I wondered if it belonged to him."

"His father had a larger house, not the mansion, but a good-sized place in the same location as Hilltop. Harold wanted to make it on his own, so he built his cabin when he was young. He moved into the new mansion he built later—Hilltop—and it wasn't too many years before a lightning bolt hit the cabin, burned it down, and that was that."

Nezzy suddenly seemed tired, and Miss Easton stepped forward.

Jessica stood. "Thank you for seeing us."

Nezzy waved her hand in reply.

The girls walked out of her room, down the long hallway with fake relatives, down the stairs, and out the front door without saying a word. When they reached the sidewalk in front of Nezzy's house, Sophie leaned against the iron fence.

"I can't believe it," she whispered.

"You were right, Sophie. There *is* a treasure."

"Shhh." Sophie glanced around. "If everyone knew what we just learned . . ."

"There'd be a stampede of treasure hunters."

"Yes. We have to keep it quiet." She held her lips together and turned them like a key. "Locked."

Jessica did the same. "Locked. Now what?"

"Today is"—she looked up as she thought about it— "Saturday! Tomorrow is Sunday. We go to the church and figure out what's in the stained glass windows. There *must* be a clue there."

17

Search the Church

Sophie sat on the end of the bed as Jessica picked up the blow dryer and stood in front of the mirror. Her cousin went through the clothes she had hanging in Sophie's closet, slipped into a light blue dress, and put on some shoes with a small heel.

Sophie rubbed her hands on her own jeans. She'd chosen her newest pair today, so they weren't faded, but maybe she should dress nicer for church. Fingering her usual ponytail, Sophie wondered if she should care more.

She walked over to her closet. There weren't many of her clothes hanging in it. You didn't need to hang jeans and T-shirts. At least she didn't. "I'd like to wear a prettier shirt to church. Could I borrow one from you?"

Jessica stopped with her brush in her hand. "I like brighter colors than you do. And girly things."

"I wore my one dress not long ago."

"You can wear anything of mine. Go through my

side of the closet." Sophie turned and saw Jessica in front of the mirror, putting on makeup. Should she try her new lip gloss?

Sophie flipped through Jessica's clothes. She could pick one of Jessica's tops and not have to wear a dress to dress up. Sorting through the tops one by one, she pushed each hanger to the side as she considcred it. Everything there was a bright color, had pretty girly things like ribbons, or both.

A shirt at the end caught her eye. It was a simple pullover, not that different from her usual T-shirts in that way, but it looked fancier. The one problem was that it was—she swallowed hard—bright pink.

After removing it from the hanger, Sophie pulled off the basic brown tee she'd put on earlier and slipped the new top on over her head. Standing beside Jessica, she checked out her reflection in the mirror.

Jessica stopped putting on makeup and watched Sophie in the mirror. "Cute."

Sophie felt that a flashing neon sign would be less noticeable. "Are you sure?"

"Oh, definitely. You're cute in it."

"Okaaay."

By the time she'd found her pair of nice shoes in the closet, the black ballet slippers her mom had bought her since Jessica had come, Sophie had decided she *might* like to look like a girl . . . sometimes. She'd gone far enough though. No lip gloss.

When Sophie stepped out of her room, her dad shouted, "Pink?"

She felt her cheeks turn the same color as the shirt. "I thought I'd look nice."

"You do. It isn't that I don't think you're beautiful in it. I think you're beautiful no matter what you wear."

Sophie hugged him. "Thanks. I'd like to get to church a few minutes early."

He rubbed his ears. "The shock from seeing you dressed up must have damaged my hearing. Did you just ask to be somewhere early?"

"Daaad."

He stared at her. "Why?"

Sophie gave what she hoped was a sweet smile. "Do I need a reason?"

He raised his eyebrows.

"Okay. We're looking for a clue."

"I have to admit that I didn't see that coming. Why would there be a clue in the church?"

"Because Mr. Laurence paid to have the church built. Maybe he made sure the builder added something that's a clue."

"That's a long shot." Smiling, he added, "I'm happy to leave early though."

As they drove, Mrs. Sandoval twisted to see the girls from the front seat and asked, "How have the cousin detectives been doing? Anything new?"

Sophie sat up straighter. "We're doing fine."

Mrs. Sandoval looked first at her, then at Jessica, with a puzzled expression.

Sophie slouched in her seat. "We're kind of stuck.

•136•

But today we're going to check out the church." She explained why.

Her dad asked, "What did Sheriff Valeska have to say about the things you found hidden in the desk?"

Sophie stared out the window. "Um, nothing."

Her dad pulled the car over to the side of the road and turned to the backseat. "Does that mean you haven't talked to the sheriff about this?"

"Yes." She turned toward him. "What would I say? 'We found hidden compartments with stuff, and we don't know if it's important'? She'd just shake her head." Sophie didn't add that she wanted to keep the hidden compartments a secret.

He stared at her for a few seconds. Then he started up the car and pulled back onto the road.

Sophie waited for a couple of minutes, then couldn't take the silence anymore. "Are you driving to the sheriff's office?"

"They're closed on Sunday."

Sophie wasn't sure if that meant she was off the hook. Or if he planned to call the sheriff at home.

Mr. Sandoval added, "I've thought about it and you're right: she probably will shake her head."

Sophie breathed a sigh of relief.

"Even so, I'd like for you to talk to her in the next couple of days and tell her what you found. It won't be you stopping by to tell her something that doesn't matter. It will be because I sent you."

Sophie nodded. "That's true. And she already knows about Mr. Jenkins."

He pulled to the side of the road again. "What about Mr. Jenkins?"

Sophie swallowed. "Um, that he isn't who he says he is."

Mr. Sandoval slowly asked, "Who is he? And I hope it's good news."

"It isn't. We overheard him." She went through the story with Jessica adding in pieces she forgot. "But we told the sheriff about that."

He let out a deep breath and started driving again. "Why didn't either you or Mandy Valeska tell us?"

"It hasn't seemed dangerous. He pretends to be nice. Maybe she didn't tell because she didn't find anything out about him."

They pulled into the parking lot beside the church.

As they climbed out of the car, Mrs. Sandoval stared up at one of the stained glass windows. "What do you girls expect to find?"

Jessica answered, "Something, anything, that appears to be a clue."

She looked down at them. "That's rather vague."

"That's the detective business, Mom."

They went up the front steps, through the doors, the small entry, and into the church. Five stained glass windows, two on each side and one at the front, rose above them, seeming to dare them to find a clue in them or somewhere else in the church. The sun pushed its way through the clouds at that moment and lit up the rainbow colors of glass.

"Wow!" Jessica said. "I never noticed how

different stained glass looked inside than out. I guess I never paid attention. It's gorgeous when the sun shines through."

They were so early that only a few other people were there, and they sat talking to each other.

Jessica leaned close to Sophie. "What should we do, just walk around and stare at each window for a while?"

Sophie said in a low voice, "Yes. But try not to attract attention to yourself."

Jessica leaned closer to Sophie. "I'm not sure that's possible, Soph. Twelve-year-olds don't usually spend much time fascinated by stained glass windows."

"Just do your best."

"I'll look at the two on the other side."

Sophie studied the first window she came to on her side. Many bright colors of glass surrounded a dove. As she stepped in front of the other window on that side of the church, this time one with the image of a man, she noticed Jessica go from a stained glass window on the opposite side to the steps that led up to the raised area at the front of the church.

When Jessica turned toward Sophie, she gestured for her to go up the stairs. Jessica looked around, probably to see if anyone was watching, and shook her head slightly from side to side. Giving one last glance at the window, Sophie went over to Jessica.

"Find anything?"

"Not that I can tell. There are lots of pieces of glass, making gorgeous pictures."

"Let's go see the one at the front of the church." She stepped forward and Jessica put her hand on her arm to stop her.

"Sophie, the church isn't empty anymore. There are *a lot* of people here."

Sophie glanced over her shoulder. Jessica was right. The pews were filling up quickly. She stared longingly at the front of the church. "I really want to see this one. It's huge and has Jesus with a man kneeling at His feet, plus lots of decorative things around them. We could find a clue in any one of those things."

"Your parents are motioning us over. We have to go sit down."

As they hurried to their seats, they saw Mrs. Bowman across the aisle, and both Sophie and Jessica leaned over to say hello.

"Hello, girls." She smiled broadly. "It was so nice to have both of you and that nice Mr. Jenkins in my bakery at the same time."

"Yes, ma'am." Sophie saw the minister going up the stairs to the pulpit.

"And he even called late yesterday to say he was relaxing on the beach and needed to order a cake for next week. So nice," Mrs. Bowman added. "Maybe your mom will send you over to buy a dessert for the family this week."

Sophie patted her shoulder and hurried to sit down. It was frustrating to be so close and not be able to see if they had a new clue. Or not. She had to keep pulling herself back to the minister's sermon.

When the service ended, her parents sat waiting for everyone else to leave. People gave them odd stares when they just sat there.

When only a handful remained, Mr. Sandoval said in a low voice, "Go to work, girls. See if there are any clues in the large window."

Mrs. Sandoval gently pushed his side. "I think you're curious too, Lucas. Why don't you walk up there with them?"

"I think I will." He winked, then followed them up the stairs. "Anything interesting, girls?"

Sophie examined the window in silence. She turned to Jessica. "Do you notice anything, Cuz?"

"I know detectives are supposed to make note of anything unusual, but I haven't studied stained glass before, so it all looks unusual to me."

"Yes. Pretty but still stained glass. Jessica, take photos with your phone. We can go over them carefully later."

Mr. Sandoval said, "You can download them to my computer so you can see them on a larger screen."

Sophie's brow furrowed. "Mom said you were working on a big project and we shouldn't bother you. Are you done?"

"I did a lot on it and am now trying to keep my work to daytime hours. I like spending the evening with your mom and you girls."

Jessica snapped photos of the glass, then stood back to get photos of the room.

Mr. Sandoval said, "Maybe the sun will come

through the window and an arrow will shine onto the wall, pointing toward the treasure."

Both Sophie and Jessica giggled.

As they started to walk out the front doors, Sophie said, "Take some photos of the entry too. And outside around the church. Let's go over everything again later."

18

After Him!

On the church steps Sophie whispered to Jessica, "I'm not sure what to do next. I wonder if Nezzy could help us more."

"I guess. Maybe." Jessica raised her hands in the air in obvious frustration. "Actually, I don't know."

"Mom, is it okay with you if we visit Nezzy? Then meet you at Great Finds?"

Her mother pulled out a key. When she started to hand it to Sophie, she paused. "Soph—"

"Moooom. You can trust me."

After hesitating for a moment, her mother dropped the key in Sophie's hand. "Let's all have lunch first. Then you can be on your way."

They went to a Greek restaurant they'd gone to before, and everyone had enjoyed. Tony and his family sat at a nearby table.

"I never thought about it, but I guess even people who own restaurants go out to eat." Jessica dipped her bread in hummus.

Mr. Sandoval stabbed a bite of his meal with his fork. "I would think they enjoy it when someone else cooks and cleans up for them."

"Just like I do when you cook dinner, Sophie," Mrs. Sandoval added.

Jessica leaned over to Sophie. "Maybe Tony could come with us today."

Sophie glanced over to his table. "He said something about doing inventory, but his whole family is there—both brothers and his sister—so maybe he isn't needed." She gave Jessica a not-too-serious glare. "Since you've told him about our mystery."

Not wanting to say enough that anyone who overheard knew about their treasure hunt, Sophie walked over to the Donadio's table and asked if Tony wanted to hang out with them for the afternoon. She gave a single wink and hoped he'd realize they wanted him to help with the mystery.

Tony grinned, said he did want to go, and both of his parents agreed.

As they left the restaurant, her parents going one way and the three of them another, Tony told them, "Whew. Thank you for getting me out of doing inventory. I don't like having to go through every single thing upstairs and in the basement and checking it off. It takes hours."

Passing a mostly empty parking lot by a doctor's office, Sophie watched a man slowly climb out of a car parked in a shady corner at the other side of the lot. As he stepped out, he glanced around constantly.

When he stood up straight, he looked their way for a second.

"Isn't that Mr. Jenkins?" Sophie turned away from the man to hide her face and pointed his direction.

Jessica squinted. "I think so. He's moving pretty quickly."

Sophie turned back. "He is now. I thought he said he was going out of town for a week."

Tony said, "Maybe he changed his plans. People do that."

"No. Mrs. Bowman told me at church that he'd called her to order a cake for next week and said he was enjoying his vacation. It's odd because he didn't act like he recognized us when he looked our way."

"He was probably thrown off by you in something other than faded jeans and a white T-shirt. I'm wearing a dress. We both look different. And Tony's dressed up too."

Mr. Jenkins glanced around one last time as he slipped into an alley.

Sophie made a split-second decision. "Let's follow him." She started in that direction.

Jessica called, "Soph, you aren't dressed for pursuit of a suspect."

Sophie noticed her cousin staring at the borrowed shirt, not at the dressier shoes.

"I know, but his being here doesn't make sense." She tugged on Jessica's and Tony's sleeves. "I'm following him. I'll be careful with your shirt, Jessica. You don't have to come if you don't want to."

Jessica rolled her eyes. "Like we'd let you chase a bad guy alone."

"We're coming." Tony added.

When they peered around the side of the building into the alley, Mr. Jenkins was ducking through a doorway toward the end of the alley.

Sophie surveyed the alley and stepped into it. Waving Jessica and Tony over, she said, "This dumpster is the only place to hide."

Jessica stopped in her tracks. Pointing at the dumpster overflowing with trash, she said, "I'm not getting in there."

"Yuck. Me neither. I can smell it from here. Let's hide beside it." She crouched in a place where she could see the door Mr. Jenkins had gone through and hoped he wouldn't leave by another door. Her cousin and Tony crouched beside her.

"Phew!" Jessica put her hand over her nose. "This place stinks. I hope we don't have to wait here very long."

After about fifteen minutes, Sophie stood. Shaking first one leg and then the other, she said, "This didn't go how I'd planned. Sneakers would be better. I'm only going to wait here another five minutes."

At that moment Mr. Jenkins stepped into the alley, glancing around just as carefully as he had before. When he walked their direction, they all jumped behind the dumpster, Sophie grimacing as her sleeve brushed against it.

Mr. Jenkins turned right at the end of the alley and

they silently followed him. One block later, he went into another alley. The girls and Tony peered around the corner and saw him exit the alley on the other side, turning left this time.

Tony said, "He's zigzagging through town like he's hiding from someone. I wonder where he's going."

"Wherever it is, we're following him there. Something's up."

"Agreed." Jessica glared at Sophie's sleeve. Sophie followed her gaze to a dirt mark. This chase might cost her a couple of months' allowance if she had to buy Jessica a new shirt.

When they reached the end of the alley, Mr. Jenkins walked quickly away from town and away from the buildings that had hidden them up to that point.

Sophie stopped and raised her hand to block the sun, noticing the color of her sleeve—the hot pink sleeve that was connected to the hot pink shirt.

Jessica pointed at the fading shape of their suspect. "We're losing Mr. Jenkins! Why aren't you following him?"

Sophie gave a frustrated groan. "I can't follow him in a shirt this color. It would be like a bright flag being waved as we walked."

"Can't you crouch low or something?" Tony asked. "There must be some way to hide."

"Even if I crawled, he'd still see a bright blob following him!"

Jessica bounced on her feet. "You're the detective.

Think of something, and *fast*. What would a famous detective do?"

Sophie spun on her heels and saw the alley behind them with new eyes. Another dumpster, this one filled with boxes, caught her eye. She ran over and grabbed a large box.

Tony and Jessica stared at her as she tucked the flaps into the box.

Tony asked, "You've had some crazy ideas before, Sophie. What on earth are you doing?"

"Let me find out if this will work. Please watch to see the direction Mr. Jenkins is going."

Jessica turned around, glancing back every minute or so. Sophie lifted the box over her head and lowered it over herself. She grabbed the underside of the box and held on, then tried to run over to Jessica, something that didn't work because the box trapped the top of her legs, and they couldn't move very quickly.

Jessica giggled. "You look like the losing entry at a costume party. We'd better hurry—if you can. Mr. Jenkins went over that hill." Jessica pointed to the left. "If I'm not mistaken, that would be the—"

"Cemetery. My guess is that he's over at Mr. Laurence's grave."

"Hold it. The cemetery? Why would he go there?" Tony asked.

"One of the weird things about our treasure hunt happened there." Sophie told him about the fresh dirt on the grave site.

"And the crow. I don't think we told you about it."

"Right. Jessica is pretty sure she saw someone dressed in black watching us."

Tony frowned. "I thought this was a nice, simple treasure hunt. Nothing like that last mystery."

Sophie started toward the cemetery, saying, "This mystery has been different. But it's anything but simple."

After just five minutes, Sophie's arms began to hurt from holding on to the box. At the entrance to the cemetery, she stopped and leaned against a tree so she could let go of it for a minute. "This *seemed* like a good idea."

"Cousin, it's probably the only thing that would work from what was lying around in an alley. And that no one would care if you used. Unless you wanted to climb into the dumpster to see what it held."

"I would for a clue."

Tony snickered. "I bet you would."

Jessica shuddered. "I'm glad you didn't have to today, for two reasons." She held up one finger. "You'd probably stink, and I'm standing next to you." Holding up another finger, she added, "And because I wouldn't even consider wearing that shirt again if you did."

Sophie pressed her lips together in a frown. "I'm not sure Mom would let me in the house without a shower." Standing upright again, she said, "Let's go."

They went into the cemetery and toward Mr. Laurence's grave.

A minute later, Sophie ducked behind a tall

gravestone, folding her knees into the box as she tried to crouch. "Someone's over there." She tilted her head to the left. "Near Mr. Laurence's grave, as I suspected. I wish we had binoculars."

Jessica pulled her phone out of her purse. "I have a binocular app on my phone. I've never tried it." She fiddled with her phone and handed it to her.

Sophie peered around the gravestone, holding up the phone. "It works. I can tell it's him, and I'm pretty sure that looks like Mr. Laurence's grave. But we're too far away even with this to tell what he's doing!"

"Let me try," Tony said.

Sophie handed the phone to Tony, and he slowly raised himself over the gravestone to be even with her. Staring at the phone, he said, "Get down! Mr. Jenkins looked up and over this way." They ducked behind the gravestone again.

Jessica fidgeted nervously. "We'd better leave, Soph. We don't want him to find us here. You move slowly with the box, and without it you stand out like a giant pink flower."

Sophie checked the time on her watch. "We also have to hurry over to Great Finds. Mom and Dad will be there in about twenty minutes, and if we aren't there, they're going to worry."

Jessica swiped her hair off her face and tucked it behind her ears. "And we might be in trouble."

Tony said, "I always try to avoid getting in trouble."

"Me too," Jessica said.

Sophie waddled like a duck, holding on to the

bottom of the box, until they were outside the cemetery. Sticking her arms in the air, she said, "Help me out of this thing."

Tony pulled the box over Sophie's head, and she shook out her arms. "I'm glad I don't have to hold on to that anymore. My arms are tired."

Tony held the box in front of himself. "We need to get out of here! Jessica, this is too big for one person to run with. Why don't you take one side of the box, and I'll take the other. We can run back to the alley where Sophie got it."

Tony, Jessica and Sophie rushed back to the dumpster to get rid of the box, then hurried over to Great Finds, arriving just in time to meet Sophie's parents, who had a surprise for them. They offered to take all three of them to a movie and already had Mr. and Mrs. Donadio's permission. Sophie didn't think twice about saying yes when she learned it was a new detective movie.

On the way home from the movie—which they'd all thought was good—they dropped Tony off. Once home, Sophie went straight to her bedroom to talk about their clues again.

Jessica picked up the photo of Hilltop and turned it in the light. "Nothing clue-like on this except maybe the photo itself. Today our clues took us away from Hilltop and to the spooky cemetery. And I thought that old mansion was spooky. By the way, thanks for letting Tony come today."

"There's safety in numbers. I'm glad we had him with us today at the cemetery. Why don't we examine the photos of the church?"

Jessica got her purse and pulled out her phone, flipping to the photos of the large stained glass windows. "These are big windows, and this is a little screen." Jessica opened the first photo and slid her fingers on the screen to make the photo larger.

Sophie leaned closer. "There are a lot of colorful pieces of glass. Make it bigger."

Jessica made the photo larger still.

Rubbing her eyes, Sophie said, "I've learned one thing from looking at these photos."

"What's that?"

"Don't ever try to look at photos of stained glass windows on a phone and expect to see little details."

Jessica set down her phone. "Good point. Your dad said we could use his computer to help with the mystery."

"Let's check with him." Sophie ran off to find her dad, but when she soon returned, her face told the story. "A client had an accounting problem, so Dad is working on it tonight. The good news is that he says he will finish this job tomorrow so we can use his computer tomorrow night."

"Excellent. We can forget about the mystery tonight."

Sophie raised one eyebrow. "You can. I'll probably be working on it while I'm sleeping."

19

Deep Trouble

The next morning, after Mrs. Sandoval had left for the antique shop, the girls had breakfast and planned their day. When it was time to get dressed, Jessica put on a sunshine yellow top and shorts. Sophie opened her dresser drawer and pulled out one of her white T-shirts and a pair of jeans. "I'm so happy to be wearing my usual clothes today. It's going to be a long time before I even *think* about wearing a box again."

"Ha! I don't think it was your style."

Sophie slowly added, "I thought it would be nice to dress like a girl, but I'm not sure that bright pink is me either," obviously hoping she wouldn't upset Jessica by saying that.

"Sophie, you look like a girl no matter what you're wearing. I *like* bright colors. You don't have to."

"That's pretty much what I decided."

"So you'll never wear hot pink again."

Sophie thought about it for a minute. "No. I think I learned that I can wear it if I want to, when *I* think it will be pretty. I don't *need* to wear that to be pretty. And I'll try to never wear the color again when I'm in the middle of a mystery."

Jessica reached out and gave her a high five, then said, "Any great ideas for this morning? We can't use Uncle Lucas' computer, and going through these photos is all I can think to do on the mystery."

"I thought we should go see the outside of Hilltop again. Maybe something on the building will stand out this time."

"We might as well. We will only have pictures of it in a few weeks." Jessica grabbed her purse. "Thinking about Hilltop reminds me of that old cabin. It's close to Mr. Laurence's house, so it's probably on his land, and we're pretty sure it's the cabin Nezzy mentioned. Maybe we should do a better job checking it out."

"Good point. The poison ivy made me a little nervous. I know there are rubber gloves under the sink." Sophie got her backpack and put two pairs of gloves inside. Then she picked up a loaf of bread and got peanut butter out of the cupboard. "Let's take lunches with us. There are some little bags of chips up there"—she pointed to a cupboard—"and some juice boxes in the fridge. Then pick something you want from the fruit bowl. I'd like an apple."

"I would too. They're just hard to bite into with braces. I'm glad your mom bought some softer fruit."

Sophie scribbled a note to her dad. Then they put the lunches they'd made in her backpack and left.

As they walked to town, Jessica said, "I just realized

the well might not be on Hilltop's land. We could be trespassing when we're there. And I really don't want to do that."

"I don't think there's a problem. Mom said that the house had thirty acres that went with it, didn't she?"

"But it doesn't have to be in a square. The thirty acres could be behind the house to the lake, out the driveway to the road, or whatever. The cabin's area does fit what Nezzy said though."

When they stopped at Great Finds to check in with Mrs. Sandoval, she didn't want them to work. Jessica noticed that she kept running her fingers through her hair like she had seen her own mother do when she was upset about something. Mrs. Sandoval listened to their plans, then said, "Just stop here about five and I'll drive you home."

When they were outside the shop, Sophie said, "Mom is usually happy. Or at least not sad."

"The Hilltop situation has gotten her down. If we find the treasure, and there's money to save the mansion, she'll cheer up."

Sophie walked on for a few minutes before she spoke again. "If we don't find something important at the cabin, let's go to the city's land office and see if they have a map of the property. It might give us a clue."

"I realized that I have a bigger, more important question."

"What's that?"

"We wandered through the woods to get out of

there. Do you have any idea where the clearing actually is?"

Sophie wavered her hand. "Yes and no. I can get us there again, but the only way I know to get there quickly without a whole lot of wandering in the woods is to go up the drive and down that path we used before."

Jessica checked all around them as they entered Hilltop's driveway.

Glancing around, Sophie said, "I don't want anyone to see us and mention to Mr. Jenkins that we were here. I haven't seen another person so far."

"Those words make me more nervous than happy."

"I know. I almost shivered after I said them."

Feeling the creepiness of the deserted road sink into her, Jessica also scanned the area. "What if Mr. Jenkins is walking down the road or is in the woods and sees us?"

Sophie chewed her lip. "I guess anything's possible, but he doesn't seem like the kind of guy to go for a nature walk. I've never seen him when I'm hiking or heard anything like that about him."

Pausing partway up the drive, Sophie said, "I want to be extra careful now that we think the cabin could be important. Let's wait a couple of minutes to see if we hear anyone coming down the road."

Sophie kept an eye on her watch. Two minutes later, on the dot, she said, "Okay. Let's move quietly down the side of the road, and jump into the woods if you hear anyone coming."

When they made the turn onto the path at the rock, Jessica looked around. "Still clear."

"I don't feel any of the spooky 'someone's watching you' kind of sensations."

"Me neither."

At the fork in the path, Sophie surprised her when they went left.

"We didn't come this way before."

Sophie said, "I know. We're close to the cabin, so I wondered if anything interesting would be over here."

Five minutes later, Jessica said, "The only interesting thing is that one path can curve around so many times. This is going to take us twice as long."

When they stepped into the clearing, Jessica gave a whoop. "I've never been so happy to be in the middle of nowhere before! At least I know where I am now. I was starting to feel lost." From Sophie's expression, she suspected she'd felt that way too, but it would take torture for Sophie to admit it.

Sophie set her backpack on a large rock. "Maybe we should eat lunch now, before we get started. It's only a little bit early."

"I always seem to be hungry when we're racing around trying to solve a mystery, so that sounds good to me." Jessica reached into the backpack and took out her lunch.

Both girls were quiet as they ate, the chips making the most noise. When Sophie pulled out her apple, she said, "Sometimes I feel like we're close to finding the treasure, and then it feels like we're pushed backward, and I'm further from solving it than I ever was."

"Me too. I guess we need to remember that people have tried to find this treasure for a very long time."

Sophie finished her lunch and stood. Rubbing her hands together, she said, "Maybe today's the day." After pulling the gloves out of her backpack, she handed a pair to Jessica, who put the last bite of her peach in her mouth before taking them. "Even with the gloves, we still need to be careful not to touch poison ivy, then touch our face or hair."

"Got it. Sophie, you, um, spent time examining the chimney last time."

"Yeah. I had to shampoo my hair three times that night to get out the eggshells and bugs. I will be happy to let you finish the chimney, and I'll take the well."

"Maybe we'll notice something one of us missed last time." Jessica moved over to the chimney and pulled back more of the vines. "Everything seems ordinary here."

Sophie walked around the well. "Here too. There are so many weeds and small bushes that they almost seem alive like they're trying to grab at my feet. Whew! One almost tripped me."

Jessica stooped to check out the lower section of the stone chimney, reminding Sophie, "Be careful. You know you can be a bit—"

"Don't say clumsy."

"Danger prone."

"I can live with that. Hey, hey—"

Jessica steadied herself against the chimney as she stood. "Sophie?"

"Help!" a voice that sounded far away cried out.

The stone suddenly shifted, and Jessica almost fell. "Sophie?" Jessica hurried around the chimney. When she saw the bottom of Sophie's shoes, with her toes hooked over the edge of the well to keep her from falling in, she raced to her. "I'm coming!"

"Hurry, Jessica! I'm holding on to a rope that's hanging inside of here. It's probably a very old, rotten rope that's going to break any second."

Jessica grabbed Sophie's ankles and sat down hard, rolling to the side as Sophie slid out of the well and landed on her bottom where Jessica had been.

"Wow. Thank you, Cousin." When Sophie stood, she grabbed for the side of the well. "Whew. I was staring at a long, dark hole and thought for a minute that I was going to find out how deep the water was."

Jessica carefully leaned over and gazed down the well. She tugged the rope toward her. "Soph, check this out."

Sophie brushed off. Then she leaned over the edge, holding onto the side. "That's a fairly new rope."

"That's what I thought, too. Someone must have changed out the rope so they could search inside the well."

"Recently."

Jessica could practically see the wheels in Sophie's mind spinning as she searched for answers.

"That might mean that Mr. Jenkins isn't sticking to

just searching Hilltop. Or someone else could be looking too. Half the town has searched for the treasure at one time or another."

"Half? I think it's more like almost every single person in town has searched for the treasure."

Sophie glanced around. "We should probably go soon. Did you find anything interesting?"

"Something is odd." Jessica went back to the chimney. "Come help me."

Sophie followed her, and Jessica pointed at the stone that had moved. "It happened right when you yelled for help."

Sophie said, "Let's pull down all the vines around it. Oh, and you can't be too careful here. Most of this is definitely poison ivy." Sophie started to reach for the stone, then stopped. "You found it. I'm going to let you pull it out. That is, if it comes out."

Jessica worked her right hand into the area that had moved and tugged on the stone. Instead of fighting her, like she thought it would, the stone shifted. "I thought it would be heavier than this, you know, like two of us might have to lift it down, but it's coming out easily."

Enough of the stone now stuck out that Jessica was able to grab it with both hands. She removed a sliver of stone, not a full block. Jessica leaned down and peeked into the hole it had left. "Wow. It only covered the front. Look what it hid."

Sophie peered inside the hole. "It's a big box." Reaching her hand in, she tried to move it. "It doesn't move. I think it's part of the chimney." She rooted around in her backpack and found her flashlight. After switching it on, Sophie pointed the light inside.

"It isn't just a box. It's a box with a *keyhole*."

Jessica peered into the hole. "A big keyhole . . . Are you thinking what I'm thinking?"

"It's like our key."

Jessica peeled off her gloves and pulled the key out of her purse. "You try it. I'm too nervous."

After peeling her gloves off too, Sophie reached into the space and put the key into the hole. "It fits. Now the question is, will it turn and open the box?" Sophie gave it a twist.

"Does it work?"

"Oh yeah. This might be the treasure." Sophie opened the door to the box and pointed the light inside. "It's empty!"

"No, it can't be empty!"

"Maybe Mr. Jenkins got here first."

"He didn't have the key."

"I really don't think that would stop someone like him."

"The box isn't damaged, so I don't think he—or whoever changed the rope—beat us to it."

Sophie reached inside. "It's still empty. There isn't anything that feels like a treasure map or diamonds or jewels." She moved her hand around. "Wait."

"Find a map?" Jessica fought against the sarcasm that tried to seep into her voice. It wasn't Sophie's fault if they discovered that the treasure couldn't be found—that someone had already found it years ago but kept it a secret.

"Not a map, but maybe a diamond." Sophie pulled her hand out of the box as a fist then opened it.

"It's a rock."

Sophie moved it in the light. "It's a white rock with gold-colored rock around it. And it sparkles. It's gold!"

"I doubt that. I think someone found the treasure in that box a long time ago. This is a joke. This whole treasure hunt is beginning to feel like a joke, and that rock is part of it."

"I'm sure it's gold, and it's important to the mystery. Let's hurry home and ask Dad."

"It's just a rock."

"Gold nugget. He may know an expert if he doesn't have the answer."

20

Clever Cody

Jessica and Sophie headed over to Great Finds a little early because Sophie planned to cheer up her mom. Mrs. Sandoval had already perked up a little. This time she smiled when they came in. Checking her watch, Mrs. Sandoval said, "I'm glad you're here early. I want to leave for home soon. I invited a family who's visiting Pine Hill over for dinner. They've stopped at Great Finds a couple of times while they've been here and seem very nice."

"Jessica and I could cook something."

"I think we'll make it easier. Run over to the deli for sides. I thawed some hamburger and won't have time to make anything fancier, but I think everyone will enjoy burgers on the grill. Sundaes will work for dessert, and I have everything for them. Tony left what he'd brought, right? You aren't planning to use the whipped cream on another project?"

"No. It's there." Mrs. Sandoval never had figured out what had happened to the whipped cream that had disappeared a few weeks ago when they'd been working on their last mystery. Mr. Sandoval must have kept their secret.

After running over to the deli for potato salad and coleslaw—buying it from Tony's older sister, since he wasn't there—they all drove home. Sophie and Jessica sliced tomato and onion while Mrs. Sandoval prepared the burgers and Mr. Sandoval put them on the grill. Just as Sophie and Jessica finished setting the table and Mrs. Sandoval was placing a vase with flowers in the center, the doorbell rang. Sophie opened the door and found the family they'd met at Hilltop standing there, with Cody in the rear. "You!"

Her mother wheeled around. "Sophie! Be polite and invite our guests, the Coopers, inside. Cody is also twelve, and Madeline is fifteen."

After the parents came in, Madeline followed, and then Cody stepped through the doorway.

Mr. Cooper chuckled. "It's okay. She and Cody, er, had a rather painful introduction."

Cody smiled, and Sophie looked as though she'd like to wipe that expression off his face. She had seemed almost ready to apologize the day of the accident, but the bruises must have annoyed her.

Cody said, "I was chased by hornets and slammed into Sophie."

Mrs. Sandoval glared at her daughter. "That could happen to anyone. Sophie, *be nice.*"

Jessica didn't like to laugh at Sophie when she was serious about something. But when she saw her cousin smile with gritted teeth before greeting the guests, she almost laughed out loud. "Welcome to our house," Sophie said. "Please come in."

As his parents sat on the couch, Cody stood next to Sophie and Jessica and said, "I really am sorry, Sophie. I stepped into a hornet's nest when we were camping last summer and got stung all over. It's made me kind of . . . nervous around hornets."

"Camping? You like to go camping?"

He nodded. "Sure. We have great camping in my part of Alaska."

"You're from Alaska!" Sophie shrieked.

Her mother popped her head out the kitchen door. "Everything all right here? Sophie?"

"Mom, they're from Alaska!"

"I know, Soph."

She pulled him over to a bench against the wall that her mother had delivered the same time as the desk. "Tell me all about Alaska."

Jessica grinned. Cody's slamming into her was all but forgotten. Learning about camping in Alaska was too good to be missed.

After dinner, Sophie said, "We can hang out on the front porch."

Jessica whispered to Sophie. "I guess we'll have to look at the photos of the church later."

She followed Sophie, Cody and Madeline Cooper walked behind her. Jessica hoped the bugs stayed away.

Sophie continued with her questions about the Coopers' home state. "Alaska sounds like so much fun. What do you do there other than camping?"

Madeline shuddered. "I don't like camping. Hiking, yes. Camping, no."

Jessica replied, "I'm with you on camping. I'm trying to like hiking."

"I'm hoping to have her loving the outdoors by the end of the summer."

Madeline asked, "What do you do here for fun?"

Sophie grinned. "We solve mysteries."

Both Cody and Madeline laughed. Cody said, "Is your mystery something difficult, like what to have for breakfast? Have you solved that one?"

Sophie said, "Earlier this summer we helped the sheriff solve a mystery."

Jessica added, "And we're hot on the trail of another mystery right now."

Cody smirked. "Right. Kids solving real mysteries."

"You can't tell anyone about what I'm going to show you. I'm only showing you now because you're visitors and can't beat us to the treasure."

"Treasure!" Cody's eyes widened, and then he laughed. When Sophie and Jessica didn't laugh too, he stared at them. "Actual treasure?"

Sophie said, "Yes."

"Okay, I won't tell."

Sophie turned to his sister.

Madeline said, "Not that I believe this, but sure."

Sophie hurried to get the clues they'd found from

her secret hiding place. When she returned a few minutes later, Jessica could see the photo, key, and rock in her hand.

"Exhibit A." Sophie held up the photo. "An old photo we found in a hidden desk drawer."

Jessica snickered.

"Hey. That's how they do it on TV." Sophie held the photo in front of each person, then handed it to Cody. "Pass it to Madeline when you're done."

Sophie reached for the key. "Exhibit B: a key we found in another hidden compartment in the desk. It opened a box behind a stone in the chimney of an old cabin that contained Exhibit C—"

Jessica interrupted. "A rock."

Sophie glared at her. Then she shrugged. "Maybe. But it's a pretty rock."

Cody held out his hand for it. As soon as it landed, he reeled back and stared at the rock. Then he picked it up and checked it from every side before carrying it over to the porch light.

Sophie stepped over to stand beside Cody. "Is something wrong?"

Cody slowly shook his head from side to side. "Where did you get this?"

Sophie cocked her head to the side. "From the box the key opened. Does that matter?"

"Maybe. I think someone hid it for a reason." He blinked and looked a little faint.

"Are you okay? Should we call your parents?" Sophie turned toward the door.

"No." Cody held up his hand. "It's just that this is *gold*."

Jessica laughed. "Sophie gets excited about things and thinks they're important. She thought it was gold too. It must be a plain old rock."

Cody said, "You don't understand. My family goes gold panning and does some dredging—that's mining. I know a gold nugget when I see one."

Jessica's mouth dropped open. Could they be close to finding the treasure?

Sophie was the first to speak. "It *really* is gold?"

Cody nodded.

Sophie's smile started small, then stretched across her face.

Jessica held out her hand, and Cody dropped the gold nugget into it. Rolling it around in her hand, she said, "I thought this was just a white rock with a gold-colored rock around it." She looked up at Cody. "Are you sure?"

"Oh, yes. It's a gold nugget. We can ask my dad, if you want another opinion."

"Wow." Sophie slumped in her chair. "We might actually find the treasure."

"This could be part of it, but this one piece of gold isn't worth a fortune. There'd have to be a lot more for it to be worth much. We could have a nice vacation if we sold this, but not buy a house or pay for college."

Sophie walked across the porch, then turned and walked back. After pausing for a few seconds, she walked the same path two more times before Jessica reached out and grabbed her wrist.

"Sit." Jessica patted the seat next to her.

As she did, Sophie said, "This is amazing. Cody, it's a good thing you visited Pine Hill this summer."

"I just wish we could stay in Pine Hill to help you find the treasure."

When their company had left, Sophie and Jessica wandered back into the house. Jessica still felt a little dazed from discovering they'd found a genuine gold nugget.

"Jessica? Hello?"

Jessica turned to Sophie. "Did you say something?"

"Yes. About five times. Do you want to go through our mystery photos on Dad's computer tonight?"

She suddenly felt tired. "Could you see if we can use it tomorrow? I need to think about what just happened."

"I do too. I'll ask Dad."

When she returned a few minutes later, she said, "He has a lunch meeting."

"Okay. We can sleep in and have fun in the morning. I'm excited about taking another look at those photos tomorrow!"

21

Stained-Glass Secrets

Just before noon, Sophie and Jessica stood in the hallway outside Mr. Sandoval's door, waiting. Seeing them there startled him when he came through the door to leave for his meeting.

"I hope you girls find the answers you want. Let me know if you see anything interesting."

"Will do, Dad!" Sophie waved to him as he went around the corner into the living room.

Jessica set her phone on the desk as they sat down in front of the computer. "Soph, do you think we're getting any closer? I know we have our clues, including the gold nugget, but we still don't know where the treasure is."

Sophie shook her head. "I wish I could say, 'Yes, we'll find it any day,' but I don't know. I do think the key Mr. Laurence left in the envelope in his desk—which started this whole mystery—means he hoped someone would search for the treasure. And the second key gave us the gold nugget in the box."

Jessica shook her head as she plugged her phone into the computer and started uploading the pictures. "I don't know. I get excited because I think we've found a great clue. Then it doesn't seem to go anywhere."

"Mr. Laurence pretty much said in that letter to Nezzy that he wanted someone to find the treasure. Are you saying that you want to give up, Jessica?"

"Are you kidding? I'm not sure we'll actually find anything, but sitting around doing nothing was seriously boring."

"I've converted you into being a fan of mysteries, haven't I?" Sophie cocked her head to the side, waiting for the reply.

"I'm not saying I love mysteries like you do, but I am having fun."

"Then let's see if anything in these stained glass windows stands out."

Jessica pulled the first photo up on the computer. "Our adventure continues."

Sophie grinned. "You have a way with words, Cousin."

"Do you think we could go to the beach later? It's a beautiful day, and I miss lying on the sand."

"I'm not sure we'll have time. We haven't even had enough time for me to mention a hike. Or camping."

Jessica clicked on the mouse.

"There's the big window at the front of the church," Sophie said, pointing at the screen. "Even though the rest of it looks like it's really old, the man in it seems modern. I wonder if he's Mr. Laurence. We've only seen small photos of him in Nezzy's book, so it's difficult to know for sure."

"There's probably a valuable portrait of him in Mr. Jenkins' room."

"I wouldn't be surprised. Anything stand out here?"

"No. Let's slowly go through them one by one." Jessica brought up those on the left side of the church first.

Sophie asked, "Do you see anything in here that doesn't seem to belong?"

"Not really. Here are the last two."

At the last window, Sophie stared, then slowly said, "Uh . . . Jessica?"

Jessica leaned closer to the screen. "What? Do you see something?"

"Keys."

Jessica glanced over at Sophie and saw her pointing at an area of the window. "Where?"

"There is a key on every window. They're almost hidden on a couple of the windows."

Jessica flipped through the photos again. "Wow. I have to pay attention on a couple of these because they're hard to find. This key is in with a bunch of flowers. That one's part of a bird's nest."

"What could Mr. Laurence be trying to tell us with keys?" Sophie went from window to window again. "The keys are all pointing toward the back of the church."

Jessica sat back in her chair. "Maybe they just wanted them to be uniform. All of the windows appear to belong together when the keys are pointing the same direction."

"Maybe, but what if Mr. Laurence was trying to tell us something?"

"I don't know, Sophie. Wouldn't the artist be the one who designed the windows?"

Sophie shook her head. "No, remember what Nezzy said? Mr. Laurence gave directions on everything he wanted in the church, including the stained glass windows."

"Sophie, I just thought of something else Nezzy said. She said Mr. Laurence was meticulous—"

"Speak English."

"He focused on details. Remember her story about the stained glass windows in the church? To him, they weren't in the right place."

"If a window wasn't put on the correct side of the church, the key in it wouldn't point to the back." Sophie's eyes got big. "Maybe the key is like an arrow and it's pointing to the treasure."

"Why not? Do you think the treasure is inside the church?"

Sophie pictured the inside of the church and the area near the windows. "I don't think so. I should really say that I *hope* it isn't there, because to say we'd get in big trouble for digging up treasure where the minister speaks is the understatement of the year."

"Maybe outside, behind the church?"

"Do you have the photos you took of the outside? Maybe we can see if anything stands out."

"Like a flashing sign that says, 'Dig here! Dig here!'?"

"Funny."

Jessica searched through the photos on the computer. "This is the back of the church where the keys seem to be pointing. I don't see anything unusual. What's in that direction if you keep going?"

Sophie squeezed her eyes shut. "I'm going to picture it in my mind. The lake's that way"—she pointed to their left. A minute later, she opened her eyes. "Trees, trees, and more trees. I don't think anyone lives there."

"Would it help you if you looked at a map of Pine Hill? Maybe you aren't seeing it all in your mind."

"You're right, Jessica. A good detective shouldn't rely on herself. She should use every tool that's available to her." Sophie went out the office door saying, "There's a map in the living room chest."

Jessica followed her and stood beside her as she opened a drawer on the chest and pulled out the map. Sophie unfolded it and laid it on the top of the chest. "Here's the church. The arrows are pointing this way." She pointed at a green part of the map.

Jessica found Hilltop on the map. "The mansion isn't far from where you're pointing."

Sophie picked up the map and held it close. Setting it down, she said, "I missed it! I'm so sorry."

"It's okay. But what did you miss?"

"Mr. Laurence's cabin and well are right under my finger on the map." She stared at Jessica.

"Wow. The keys in the church windows *are* pointing at the old cabin."

"Yes. We found the nugget there, so we found the clue he was pointing to even before we found the arrows. I think we're closer to the treasure than anyone else has ever been."

Jessica took a deep breath. "I think you're right. Let's make sure we haven't missed anything in the stained glass." She hurried back to Mr. Sandoval's office.

Again in front of the computer, Jessica flipped through the images.

"Stop." Sophie pointed. "This window shows a well and a woman. The woman looks a little like Nezzy when she was younger."

"Right! Sophie, I only remember seeing one well the whole time we've been on this mystery."

Sophie hopped to her feet. "I've had a couple of nightmares about falling into that well, so believe me, I can picture it clearly. Maybe if we tell all of this to the sheriff, she'll take us seriously and work with us to find the treasure."

"We've seen keys and more keys since the beginning of this case. There was one in the envelope, another one in the desk, one on the brick."

"I feel like we've seen something about a key somewhere else." Sophie tapped her foot as she thought. "Where else did we see one?" She snapped her fingers. "The word *key* was on Mr. Laurence's gravestone. And someone wanted to hide the stone that had that word. Do you think that's important?"

"Until we find the treasure, I'm going to assume everything is important."

"I'm surprised I'm saying this, but let's go back to the cemetery."

22

Stakeout Tonight?

When the girls neared the cemetery, sunshine made everything bright, but Sophie felt like turning around and heading the other direction. Still, she continued on, moving quickly, checking over her shoulder every minute or two. She couldn't put her finger on why, but she felt something wasn't right.

Sophie said, "At least we know where Mr. Laurence's grave is now. We don't have to spend extra time searching for it.

Jessica answered. "Yes. I know exactly where I'm going in a cemetery. That's more than a little weird."

When they neared the place she was sure it lay, Sophie said, "I guess I'm wrong. That can't be his grave. The grass is dug up all around it."

"No, this is it. See? The name is right." Jessica pointed at the tombstone.

"Jessica, it can't be. It looks like—"

They both jumped back and looked around.

Sophie whispered, "Someone's been digging

around here. I'd guess at night, so no one can see them."

Jessica gulped and whispered, "Yes. I'm glad we have a little while before it's nighttime. Let's get out of here!"

As they hurried away, Sophie said, "Wait! We didn't read the words on that stone again, to make sure it did say something about a key." She started to turn back, but Jessica grabbed her arm and pulled her forward.

"We aren't turning back. We can return tomorrow. Maybe with the sheriff."

They ran all the way into town, then stopped, panting and leaning against the front of Kendall's Jewelers.

"Jessica"—Sophie stopped to catch her breath— "someone's probably searching for the treasure around Mr. Laurence's grave. I don't know why, because I don't think it's there."

They stared at each other.

"Mr. Jenkins!" Jessica whispered.

"And Lester. They must be desperate to dig around a grave. I'm pretty sure the word *key* was on the stone, but—"

"He must have learned about the keys somehow. Maybe he heard us talking. I wonder if he's checking everything that has something to do with a key."

"That's stupid. Mr. Laurence couldn't put something there, not in his own grave."

"Maybe they aren't as smart as we thought."

"They're probably just desperate to find the treasure. Hilltop will be torn down soon, and Mr. Jenkins' reason to be in Pine Hill will be gone."

"They might be back tonight."

Jessica gasped. "You're right. Maybe we'd better stop at the sheriff's office."

"Good idea. We'd better hurry so we catch her before she leaves for the day."

Once they could see the sheriff's office, they could also see someone getting into a sheriff's car parked at the curb. "That's her!" Sophie started to run, but the car pulled out and headed down the street.

"So much for that idea! Let's get over to Great Finds before Mom wants to leave for the day too."

When they arrived at the shop, Sophie was surprised to see her dad standing inside.

"A customer arranged with your mother to come in after she usually closes," he said. "I'm driving both of you home." As they stepped out the door, he added, "You barely made it before it started to get dark."

"But we *did* make it." Sophie gave her best smile.

The sun set as they drove. As they pulled into the driveway, an idea came to her. Her dad got out and went inside, but she pulled Jessica aside. "If someone's digging at night, maybe we should be there, watching to see who it is."

"Right. We're going to ask your parents if we, two twelve-year-old girls, can spend the night in a cemetery, waiting for someone who has the guts to dig around a grave."

Sophie couldn't see Jessica clearly in the fading light but knew from her tone of voice that she must have rolled her eyes.

"I see your point." Sophie scrunched up her mouth, thinking, then said, "What if Tony, Cody, and Madeline came along?"

"Oh, so now we have five kids."

"I hate it when you're this right. Let's ask Dad if he will come with us."

When they stepped inside, Sophie asked, "Dad, will Mom be home for dinner?"

He didn't look up from reading a book. "Yes, she expects to be here in about an hour."

Sophie pulled Jessica into the kitchen. When the door closed, she said quietly, "This might be a good night for us to cook dinner. Mom will be happy to have it taken care of, and Dad might be happier about helping us."

"What are you going to cook?"

"Let's check the fridge and see if I can figure out what she was planning to make."

Ten minutes later, they'd started cooking sausage and put spaghetti sauce on to heat.

Jessica stirred the sauce, which was beginning to bubble. "It always amazes me when you are able to make something that tastes good."

"Mom's been teaching me to cook for years." Sophie pulled veggies out of the fridge. "Would you like to fix salads?"

"Just tell me what to do."

"Put lettuce in four bowls. Cut everything into bite-sized pieces. Done."

Jessica peeled and very carefully cut up the veggies. "I've had dried cranberries and pecans in a salad."

"If you find it in the kitchen, go for it."

Sophie took a metal pot out of the cupboard and put water in it for cooking pasta. She had just placed it on the stove when her mom came in the front door and called to them. Sophie answered and her mom stepped into the kitchen. "Making dinner?"

"Yes."

"Thank you, Sophie." She hugged her. "And Jessica." She reached over and hugged her too. "I had a busy, long day, and I'm so happy you're making dinner that I won't ask what you want until after dinner."

As Mrs. Sandoval put her hand on the kitchen door, Sophie said, "It's easy and won't cost anything. Don't worry."

"Music to my ears. I'm going to kick off my shoes and wait for whatever it is you're cooking." She went out the door.

When Sophie and Jessica brought the sauce with sausage, pasta, and salads to the table, Mr. and Mrs. Sandoval were seated there waiting for them.

After topping her pasta and sauce with Parmesan cheese, Sophie took a bite of the meal. "This is good. If I say so myself."

Mrs. Sandoval took a bite and sighed. "I'm glad I taught you to cook. You've made a delicious dinner."

When Sophie started to speak, her mother held up her hand. "Wait until we're done."

As Mrs. Sandoval put the last bite in her mouth, Sophie said, "We have a little favor we'd like Dad to do." She took a big breath and smiled sweetly at her father. "We'd like for you to go with us to the cemetery tonight."

Silence. Mr. Sandoval stared at her. "Cemetery? Dare I ask why?"

Sophie explained what they'd found.

"Why were you there today in the first place?"

"Keys. We found keys in the stained glass windows at the church. We've found keys over and over again on this mystery. And the word *key* is on a stone that sits on Mr. Laurence's grave."

Jessica jumped in and described the keys in the stained glass.

Mrs. Sandoval asked, "And they seem to be like arrows?"

Sophie sat tall in her chair and said confidently, "They are arrows pointing to the woods beside Hilltop."

Jessica cleared her throat. "They *appear* to be arrows."

"They're arrows. What else would they be?"

"Don't get me wrong, Soph. I think they're arrows too. I'm just not certain."

Her dad jumped in. "No matter what they are and what they're pointing to, I don't believe we should check out a 'key' at the cemetery—"

"Daaad!"

"—without the sheriff or a deputy," he continued. "I'll call and see if someone can come."

"Thanks!"

Mr. Sandoval arose, walked over to the phone, and dialed. When someone answered, the girls listened to his side of the conversation. He hung up a minute later.

"There's a conference the sheriff and most of the deputies are at, over in the county seat. No one can go with us tonight."

Sophie sagged in her chair.

He added, "The deputy on duty said he'd tell the sheriff and ask her to call if she has a chance."

Mrs. Sandoval stood. "Girls, I've had time to relax now because of the dinner you made. I'll do the dishes."

Sophie didn't feel as happy as she should that she didn't have to do the dishes. They *had* to solve the mystery. She got up from her chair and slowly went to her room with Jessica beside her.

"Don't worry, Soph. We'll get to look tomorrow. Let's read. It'll make you happier."

Sophie flopped back on her bed. "We may miss something tonight."

"Relax. There isn't anything we can do about it."

Sophie lay there and didn't even pick up her book.

When the phone rang a few minutes later, Sophie ran to the living room to answer it with Jessica on her heels. She covered the mouthpiece of the phone and whispered, "Sheriff Valeska." A frown turned down the corners of her mouth. "No, it isn't an emergency. But—but—are you sure? . . . Okay." She slowly set the phone on its cradle.

Mr. Sandoval asked, "My guess is that she can't come tonight."

"She's the speaker at a dinner for sheriffs that's about to start, so she said 'nothing short of an emergency' can have her back in Pine Hill tonight."

Her dad picked up the newspaper. "I guess there's nothing else to do about it."

"She said she'd have a deputy drive through the cemetery every hour."

He settled on his chair. "You can stop by the sheriff's office in the next day or two."

Sophie put a hand on her chest. "You don't understand mysteries, Dad. We can't let this clue go cold. She said she'd be in the office in the morning, so we'll stop by then—if it's okay with you."

When they got back to Sophie's room, she did pick up her book this time, but laid it beside her on the bed after a few minutes. "I can't focus on reading," she told Jessica. "I've been going over clues in my mind. I feel like we should have all the clues we need to find the treasure."

"But they aren't connecting in your mind?"

"Exactly!"

"That's how I feel too." Jessica set her book on the nightstand. "I have no idea what's going on in this chapter either."

"We have keys, gold, and a photo. Are the keys on the stained glass important, or did Mr. Laurence just like keys? Does the well in the stained glass matter? We already found the gold nugget at the cabin site." Sophie blew out a long breath in frustration.

The phone rang again, but she didn't get up.

"Soph! Jessica!" Mr. Sandoval called a minute later. He leaned in the doorway to Sophie's room. "The sheriff just phoned to say she'd finished her speech and could come back if it was important. I explained what you'd found and she decided to do a stakeout at the cemetery. We can meet her there in an hour."

"Yay!" Sophie pumped her fist in the air. "Now, let's call Tony and the Coopers."

Mr. Sandoval stood straight. "Why do we need all these people, Soph? Sheriff Valeska agreed to do the stakeout and allow *you and Jessica* to see it—from a distance."

"Due to a slip by my cousin"—Sophie gave Jessica a look—"Tony's been involved in this for a while. I don't think he'd be happy about missing the stakeout. And Cody's the one who told us it was gold. Madeline might like to come too."

When Mr. Sandoval walked away, Jessica whispered, "And Cody's cute."

Sophie grinned and whispered back, "And he's cute."

Once her dad had had enough time to make the phone calls, she stepped over to the door to her room. "How's it going, Dad?"

"The Donadios were easy to reach and gave approval—since Sheriff Valeska's going to be there. The Coopers haven't answered."

Sophie came back and slumped onto her bed. "There are so many pieces to this mystery. And now that we think we're finding answers, we have to get all of the parents to agree."

A few minutes later, her dad stepped into her room. "Let's go, Soph! I finally reached the Coopers. You know how cell phone reception is in town. Madeline didn't want to come, but they're on their way to drop Cody off at the sheriff's office. The sheriff said to drop you two off—Tony's meeting us there—and she'd take you all to the stakeout."

"Yay!" Sophie bounced to her feet. She pulled her flashlight out of her nightstand drawer. "Let's go, Jessica."

"I wish I could be as happy as you are about going to a cemetery at night."

"I won't say we'll have fun, but I think we might see who's doing this. If that person is caught, they might know something about the treasure."

"And you think they'll tell us what they know? Sure. They won't want to get the treasure themselves. They'll be happy to share their information."

"There's no need to be sarcastic." Sophie stopped with her hand on the light switch. "There may be some truth in what you say, but I won't let go of my happy feeling. *This* is the night we've been waiting for."

23

Grave Danger

Sheriff Valeska unpinned her badge, the shiny metal glinting in the moonlight. As she tucked it into her pocket, she said, "Reflective metal and a full moon aren't a good combination. We don't want to alert anyone before they're in our trap." Then she motioned for them to follow her. On the other side of the cemetery, she pointed to a large carved angel. "This is big enough for all four of you to hide behind."

Sophie turned to her. "Sheriff? We'll miss all of the action if we're over here."

"What you'll miss is the danger. Can you see what's happening from here?"

"Yes, but—"

"Could you see the action from your house?"

Ooh. Jessica watched Sophie's quick reaction and bit her lip to hide a grin.

"This is a great spot. Thanks, Sheriff."

Sheriff Valeska gave one curt nod. "I'm glad you agree."

As they crouched behind the headstone, Jessica said, "Soph, seeing the sheriff's badge reflect in the moonlight brought back a part of the case that we pushed aside. There's the original story of the doctor seeing Mr. Laurence in the woods and the moonlight reflecting off of gold."

Sophie brushed the idea away. "No, we decided that couldn't be true. Besides, where would a whole bag of gold be?"

"We should tell Tony and Cody about the windows in the church."

After Jessica told the story, Cody said, "If the well in the window is a clue to lead us to the old well . . ."

Sophie said, "It has a key on a stone, but it's just a stone, and it seems like someone searched down inside the well already. The gravestone has a sentence on it that includes the word *key*, so maybe all of the words on it do mean something more."

"Yes, you're right." Jessica settled down to wait.

Tony said, "Don't you think the arrows in the stained glass are pointing to the treasure?"

"We already checked there." Sophie fought against the sarcastic comment she wanted to make.

"I think we can *conclude*—" He glanced over at Sophie. "Does that sound like detective language to you?"

She nodded.

"We can conclude that the well has to be where the treasure is. You somehow missed it."

Sophie added, bouncing up and down on the

ground, "Everything that had a key on it was important. We'll go check the well again in the morning. And you can come if you want." She softly punched Tony in the arm.

Jessica could see the glint of moonlight off his teeth when he smiled.

All of them settled into the stakeout, finding their positions behind the angel.

A short time later, bushes behind them rustled. Sophie checked their group. Everyone was there; Tony and Cody were chuckling about something, and Jessica was focused on the sheriff's hiding place. She nudged Cody and whispered, "Did you hear that?"

"What?" Cody asked.

"Bushes moving," Sophie said.

"You're imagining things." He laughed quietly, then leaned over and said something to Jessica.

Sophie stared over her shoulder. Could she have imagined it? Even if the bushes had moved, it could have been a possum or another harmless nighttime animal. She heard another rustle. The other three were talking in low voices about something. She quietly slipped into the bushes to see what was going on.

Jessica stopped talking and focused on the stakeout. The warm summer air hung still and nothing moved, not even a mouse. She turned to Sophie to make a joke about it, but she wasn't there. Jessica looked all the way around them.

When she leaned to the right to check for Sophie on the other side of the angel they hid behind, Tony asked, "What are you doing?"

She whispered, "Sophie's gone!"

Cody heard her too, so both boys checked the area. Cody asked, "Is this something she does, vanish?"

Jessica said, "Absolutely not. I don't understand where she could be." When the bushes rustled, she added. "I'm glad we're getting a breeze, anyway. It's so still, it's eerie."

Cody held his hand in the air. "There is no breeze."

Branches breaking and leaves rustling made them all turn to look.

"Sophie?" Jessica whispered. Then she said her name a little louder.

Tony stood. "This isn't like Sophie."

A crashing sound brought the rest of them to their feet. A muffled voice sounded. Then silence.

Jessica's voice quivered, "Do you think that was Sophie calling for help?"

Cody shook his head. "If it was, I don't think she got to finish what she was trying to say."

A new crashing sound pushed through the woods, moving away from them.

Cody cleared his throat. "My guess is that Sophie was just taken away by someone who was hiding in the woods."

Jessica gasped. She took a step toward the sheriff, but Tony grabbed the back of her jacket.

He said, "Remember, Sheriff Valeska said they

would be ready to grab anyone who walked into their trap."

"Then what?"

Cody said, "Let's shout at her."

Jessica said, "Great idea, Cody. On three, shout . . . What do we shout?"

Tony jumped in. "'Criminal!' And point the way the noise went."

Jessica said, "One, two, three!"

When they all shouted, Sheriff Valeska stepped out from where she was hiding and hurried over to them. Scowling, she asked, "What are you doing?"

Jessica said, "Sophie's missing. And we heard footsteps running away."

"Over here!" the sheriff called to her deputies. "Bring all the lights."

Three deputies hurried over with the gear.

"Please tell me what happened, Jessica," the sheriff ordered her.

After she'd finished, Cody added, "I just remembered. She told me she'd heard bushes rustling . . . I'm sorry, but I thought she was imagining things."

The sheriff sent her deputies into the woods to search. Jessica felt like time barely moved as they waited for some sign of Sophie.

A couple of minutes later, a deputy called, "Sheriff, check this out."

Cody, Tony, and Jessica followed the sheriff into the woods.

A shovel lay on the ground, and the powerful lights

showed an area where the plants had been flattened. The sheriff crouched and said, "It looks like something, or someone, was pulled for a few feet. Then there are only normal footsteps." She turned to Jessica, Tony, and Cody. "I'll get a deputy to drive you home. We'll find her. Don't worry."

When she turned away, Jessica said, "No, Sheriff. Wait. I know where they're going."

"Where? How do you know?"

"Well, I should say I'm pretty sure I know where they're going. I mean, why would they go anywhere else?"

"Jessica, you're babbling. Take a deep breath."

Jessica obeyed. Then the sheriff said, "Now, slowly tell me what you mean."

"We—that is, Sophie and I—found an old well in the woods, and we believe the treasure is there."

"That's sounds like a good idea, Jessica, but the criminals wouldn't know to go there."

"Actually, they would. We talked about it when we were settling into the stakeout. If they were in the woods, then . . ."

Sheriff Valeska turned to Cody, "Right after that is when Sophie heard the rustling bushes?"

"Yes, ma'am."

"I don't know of a place like you're describing, Jessica. Could you take us there?"

Jessica stared down at the crushed leaves, probably crushed by Sophie struggling to get away from someone. She needed her help. "Yes, I can take you there. The only way I know is down a path leading from Hilltop's driveway."

The sheriff rounded up her team. Once gear was returned to trunks, she ushered Jessica, Cody, and Tony into her vehicle and took off for Hilltop with two more squad cars following close behind.

When they turned in to Hilltop's drive, Jessica said, "Go slowly. I have to find some boulders next to the road."

"There?" The sheriff pointed out the window at the large rocks. When Jessica nodded, she stopped the car. Sighing, she said, "I wish I could tell you to stay in the car, but I need Jessica to show us the way. You may as well all come. But Cody and Tony, please stay to the rear. And Jessica, once we're there, you step to the rear too."

The four of them got out of the car. As they started down the trail with the other officers who had followed them there, the sheriff added, "Everyone, deputies included, walk softly and don't speak. We want to do our best to surprise them."

Jessica recognized the twisted tree and whispered to the sheriff, "We're almost there."

Sheriff Valeska pulled the three of them aside and whispered, "You three kids stay here. I'm leaving a deputy with you." In a voice only slightly louder, she said to the rest of the group, "Lights off, everyone."

A woman who quietly introduced herself as Deputy Story stood beside them as the others continued out of sight.

Jessica waited for sounds of a rescue. She pulled her phone out to check the time and kept checking it every few minutes. Eleven minutes of waiting brought the sheriff back to them.

She spoke in a normal voice. "I'm sorry, Jessica, but they aren't at the well."

"They have to be here. This is the one place they would want to go." She stared up at the sky. "I know! *If* they haven't been here before—and that's a big if—Sophie's taking them on a roundabout trip so we can get here first."

The sheriff pondered that silently. "With anyone else, I'd say that's ridiculous. No one would spend more time with kidnappers than they had to."

"That's how Sophie thinks, though."

"I was about to say that too. Follow me. Let's all hide in the woods and wait for them."

She explained to her deputies what was going on, adding, "Everyone wait for my signal. I'll shine my light in the eyes of the man holding Sophie."

They were soon hidden in a circle around the well, with Tony, Cody, and Jessica together at the rear, the farthest point from the trail. Jessica made sure they hid in grass, *not* in poison ivy.

24

Setting a Trap

Sophie hoped she'd delayed the criminals long enough. She didn't think they'd be very nice if she delayed them any longer. Her heart had raced so much when they'd captured her that she'd thought it would burst through her chest. Then she'd calmed herself down. She knew what she had to do to get rescued and stop the criminals, all at the same time. But she didn't see a way out of this if the sheriff wasn't at the well.

Lester, the man who seemed to be in charge, said in a gruff voice, "This better be it. You took a long way around to get to the trailhead."

"I'm a kid. I'm not used to trying to spot things from a car at night."

"You'd better not be leading us down the wrong path." Lester poked her in the arm and made her yelp, then said, "Hey, keep it quiet, kid."

"You hurt me."

Mr. Jenkins said, "Lester, leave the kid alone. It

doesn't matter if she makes noise anyway, because I don't think we're near anything but trees."

They stepped into the clearing and a third man said, "Boss, we're here." He shined a light around the area. "There's a well over there."

Lester said, "So there is." Pulling Sophie in front of him, Lester tugged her over to the well. "Show me where to find the treasure."

Sophie said, "Let me see it more closely," and crouched in front of the well.

Immediately a bright beam of light flashed on, and Sophie dropped flat to the ground as deputies surged into the clearing, tackling the three criminals. The sheriff herself rushed to help Sophie to her feet. "Are you okay?" she asked.

"I knew, or at least I hoped, you'd come here, and I wanted you to be ready and waiting when we got here."

The sheriff hugged her. "That was smart, Sophie."

"There's something about being captured by bad guys that makes you smarter."

"How did they get you?"

"I guess I didn't start out smart. I heard a noise in the bushes and went to check it out. Three men were hiding in there, listening to us. I thought I could sneak back to the others, but I stepped on a branch, so they knew I was there. When one of the men grabbed hold of me, I tried to call for help, but he covered my mouth. I fought to get away, but they pulled me with them." She took a deep breath. "They had a shovel and had planned to dig more at the grave. But they heard us talking about the well."

Officers had already cuffed two of the men. As the deputy was about to click Mr. Jenkins' handcuffs into place, he shoved the officer to the ground and tore off into the woods.

"Run after him!" Sophie yelled and took off with Tony, Cody, and Jessica right behind her.

"No!" the sheriff yelled. "You kids get back here right—" But before she could finish her sentence, Tony tackled the fleeing man, grabbing his ankles. Cody pinned his arms behind his back.

"Football," Tony said, grinning at Cody.

"Wrestling." Cody grinned back.

When all three men were handcuffed, Sheriff Valeska turned to Sophie. "People have looked for this treasure for a hundred years. How do *you* know where it is?"

"It has to be here, sheriff. The keys point this way."

"Keys? You're going to have to explain that to me more clearly when we're done here."

The sheriff inspected the well, walking around it and shining the light inside. "I've seen other old wells, Sophie. This one doesn't appear different. A bag of gold is rather large. Where would Laurence have hidden it?"

Sophie knelt in front of the well and the brick with the key on it. "I don't know, Sheriff. I just know it has to be here. Other than being larger than the other stones, the stone with the key on it doesn't look unusual. Of course, it's very grimy and covered with bits of vine." In exasperation, she pushed on it, but the stone was solidly in place like those around it. "They sure built things well in the old days."

The sheriff agreed. "I don't see anything here, Sophie. We'll take these men in for the night, and figure out what to do in the morning."

Sophie kept staring at the stone. The sheriff turned away, then said, "You're going with us."

Sophie knew she didn't have any choice. "Okay."

Sheriff Valeska drove them to her office where they called Mr. Sandoval to pick them up.

While he drove them home, they took turns telling him what had happened. Tony and Cody spoke first, each telling as much of the story as he could before being dropped off, Tony at home and Cody at a campground. They were almost home themselves when Jessica, who was telling the story at that point, got to the part about Sophie.

Mr. Sandoval yelled, "What?! Are you okay, Soph? Tell me the truth."

"Yes. They didn't hurt me, Dad. Well, my wrist feels bruised, but that's all. I'll admit that it was scary, but I'm fine. More or less. Kind of." She paused. "Let's just say that I'm glad we're going home and that those men are locked up."

When they arrived home and her mother heard the story, she hurried Sophie off to a warm bath.

Like that would somehow fix everything.

25

The Final Key

The next day when Jessica woke up, Sophie wasn't in bed. She pulled on her robe and went into the shower knowing that this morning she needed to wake up fast. She had a feeling that being groggy and grumpy wouldn't be optional.

After showering and drying her hair, Jessica put her robe back on and left the bedroom to hunt down Sophie. She found her in the kitchen, holding a mug.

Sophie looked up and smiled. "Hot chocolate."

"In the summer?"

"Mom seems to think that hot baths and hot chocolate are good for you."

Jessica grabbed a couple of slices of bread and popped them in the toaster. "Is she right?"

"She might be. I did feel better after I sat in the hot bathtub last night." Smiling, she added, "I'm not sure about the hot chocolate, but I do know that I like it. It may be the only chocolate that I really like."

"Want some toast?"

Sophie looked down at the mug. "I guess this isn't much of a breakfast. Sure."

Jessica buttered the toasted bread and pulled a jar of peanut butter from the cupboard, handing both to Sophie before she popped two more slices in the toaster for herself.

"I guess the mystery is over, Sophie. We did everything we knew to do. Even the bad guys thought we were right, but the treasure wasn't there."

Sophie dropped her toast on the plate and hugged the mug closely with her hands. "I know. I just feel inside"—she tapped her chest—"that the treasure is at the well. It has to be there. Everything points to it."

Jessica sat at the table, slathered peanut butter onto her toast, then nibbled thoughtfully. "The sheriff's right. Where can it be?"

"I don't know." Sophie set the mug down with a thud. "I'm frustrated. When I picture it in my mind, all I see is a well made up of a bunch of stones."

"Yes. They're all approximately the same size and shape. Except for the stone with the key on it."

Sophie paused with the toast almost to her mouth. "What if that means something? Could you hide something inside a rock? Maybe he carved out the center and poured the gold nuggets inside."

Jessica shook her head. "It wasn't big enough to hold a bag of gold nuggets."

Sophie stood. "Let's go there this morning. I want to see it one last time before I completely give up. I've never given up on a mystery before."

Jessica felt like pointing out that this was only the second mystery they'd worked on, so she'd only solved one. Instead, she told her, "I'll go with you. One last time. Now that I know the only other people seriously looking for the treasure are locked up."

After asking Mr. Sandoval if they could go, they walked silently to town and over to Hilltop's entrance. A few minutes up the road, they turned onto the path to the cabin. Trudging along through the woods, Jessica wondered if this was yet another waste of time.

Sophie first spoke when she saw the well. "It's here. I know the treasure's here."

"Maybe someone found it years ago. If they found it, they might not have wanted to share with family and friends."

"That's true." Sophie studied the ground around the well. "I wonder if we should try digging here?"

"I'm not sure that's a good idea with the big, deep hole of the well so close by. What if it all collapsed?"

"Right."

It wasn't like Sophie to agree with everything Jessica said. Her cousin definitely wasn't herself this morning.

Sophie knelt in front of the key stone again. "That one's so different from the others. It isn't even the same texture."

Jessica crouched beside her. "The other stones have the appearance of being chiseled out of solid rock with a hammer. This one is almost smooth." She ran her hand over the surface. "It's so smooth that it looks modern, like it was made in a mold, not carved by hand."

As Sophie stared at it, her eyes got bigger and bigger. Jessica wondered if she was having an attack of some kind. "Are you okay? Sophie?" She reached out and shook her. "Are you okay?"

A laugh started low, then grew, until Sophie sat back on the ground, holding on to her sides.

Jessica pulled her phone out of her purse, hoping it would pick up a signal. Sophie obviously needed help.

Her cousin reached out and touched her arm. "I'm not going crazy," she choked out. "It's just that it's there." She pointed at the key stone.

Jessica stared first at the stone, then at her cousin. "Okaaay," she said slowly.

Sophie searched the ground around her, picked up a small rock and then another, before choosing one. She got back on her knees in front of the key stone and scraped against it with the rock. "I knew it!" She pointed at the mark she'd made.

Jessica shrugged. "It's still a rock, one with an ugly scrape on it, but still a rock."

"Get closer."

Jessica decided to humor her. The faster they got out of here, the better. Sophie moved to the side so Jessica could get a few inches from the stone. A metal color glimmered out from the scrape. "Sophie, hand me your rock."

Sophie held out her hand and Jessica took the rock and made another scrape, even larger, beside the first one. Jessica gasped. "You found it!"

"When you said it seemed like it was made in a mold, it all came together in my mind. Mr. Laurence melted the gold in the shape of a stone. That's probably what he was doing the night the doctor saw him. Then he painted it the same color the other stones are naturally. The gold has been here at the well all along."

Both Jessica and Sophie stood.

Staring at the rock, now with grooves glinting in the sun, Sophie said, "*We* did it! Let's go tell the sheriff."

They raced to town and over to the sheriff's office. When they burst through the door, Sheriff Valeska jumped. "What are you kids doing here? We settled everything last night."

Sophie glanced over at Jessica, then grinned and walked over to the sheriff. "We found it. We found the gold."

A male voice said, "*Sure*, you did. *I* never found it, but two kids found it today."

The girls both spun to the right and found Mr. Jenkins sitting in a chair wearing handcuffs. Jessica figured they must have been questioning him or something like that.

"Sophie, I'm tired." They turned back to face the sheriff, who rubbed her hands over her face. "We were out fairly late, and I had an early call this morning. There is no treasure."

"Yes, there is. Remember the stone with the key on it?"

The sheriff nodded. "I'll humor you. Yes, I remember the stone. You said the treasure had to be there."

"It is. The stone isn't a stone. It's gold."

The sheriff came to her feet. "Are you sure?"

"I can vouch for her, Sheriff. She scraped it with a sharp rock and I saw gold."

"What?!" Mr. Jenkins yelled. "I searched for the treasure for almost fifteen years, put up with everything this small town had to offer, smiling the whole time, and these kids found it?"

Sophie crossed her arms over her chest. "Yes."

He motioned them over to his chair. "Tell me, did you actually find the bag of gold?"

"He melted it into a block."

"Melted?" He sat back in the chair, head in his hands, muttering softly, "Melted," over and over again as they went back to the sheriff's desk.

The sheriff was hanging up the phone. She asked, "Sophie and Jessica, do you want to be there when we remove the gold block from the well? We have an expert with bricks and stone coming to help."

"Of course," they said at the same time.

When the sheriff laughed, Sophie said, "You already knew the answer."

"Of course I did. I was having fun with you. And I'd ask if someone was pretending to be you if you'd answered no. Let's all go in my car. Notice I *didn't* ask if you wanted to do that. I do have one stop to make."

On the way, Jessica asked, "Do you have any idea how much the gold is worth?"

"We have an estimate based on the size of the stone, as I remembered it from last night, but we won't know for sure until it's weighed."

After a long stop at the site of a car accident, they got to the well. Two deputies were there, along with an expert, who was already at work on the gold block.

Jessica stood to the side and watched him. "I wondered how you would do this."

The expert said, "I've chiseled out the mortar on the edges. We should be able to remove it soon."

Sophie stood on the other side of him. He pointed upward. "We have an old-fashioned block and tackle set up. A pulley system to lift this." He slid a thin wire under the block and used it to pull through another piece that acted like a sling. Then he clipped that onto the rope that hung from the pulley.

His men pulled on it, and the stone rose. Two sheriff's deputies placed the stone in a duffle bag, and each took a handle, carrying it to the sheriff's car with everyone following behind them. One of the deputies got in the passenger seat, and the girls climbed in the backseat.

Jessica said, "I think Mr. Laurence would like to know that the gold was used for something good."

Sheriff Valeska said, "It will be. This was found on Hilltop property, so it belongs to the city. The house will be saved and still be here, Sophie and Jessica, when you're as old as Nezzy Grant."

Two days later, when the girls stepped onto the sand at Pine Lake's beach, Jessica felt the stress from the last couple of weeks slide away. "*Yes.*" She sighed. "We finally got to the beach. Now that the bad guys are all locked up."

Sophie put her towel on the sand. "It did turn out well, didn't it?"

"Uh-huh. But I don't want to talk about it. I want to pretend that we never found a criminal in Pine Hill." Jessica placed her towel beside Sophie's and stretched out on it. "Maybe we can avoid mysteries for the whole day."

"After I say this—"

Jessica groaned. "No! Please."

"We found the treasure, saved Hilltop with the huge amount of money the gold was worth, and escaped the bad guys. You wrote an article about the mystery for the newspaper."

"All true and very good. I like writing for the paper, and I'm especially relieved that you escaped from Mr. Jenkins, Lester, and their friend." Jessica put her hands over her ears. "But I need a break from mysteries."

Sophie pulled Jessica's hand away from her right ear and leaned closer. "I just wanted to say that our last mystery turned out well, so maybe our next one will be even better."

If you haven't read
The Feather Chase, don't
miss the exciting
beginning of
the Crime-Solving
Cousins Mysteries!

One More Mystery

Sophie and Jessica found a rope that looked new inside the well. Who went to the well before them and why were they there?

Unscramble each word and put them together to make a sentence that gives you the answer.

SSMI _M_ _i_ _s_ _s_

AKREWL ___ ___ ___ ___ ___ - ___

DTENAW _w_ _a_ _n_ _t_ _e_ _d_

OT _T_ _o_

NFID _F_ _i_ _n_ _d_

ETH _T_ _h_ _e_

OLGD _G_ _o_ _l_ _d_

_____

_____

Answers at www.shannonlbrown.com

About Shannon

Writing books that are fun and touch your heart

Even though Shannon L. Brown always loved to read, she didn't plan to be a writer. She earned two degrees from the University of Alaska, one in journalism/public communications, but didn't become a journalist.

Years passed. Shannon felt pulled into a writing life, testing her wings with a novel and moving on to articles. Shannon is now an award-winning journalist who has sold hundreds of articles to local, national, and regional publications.

The Feather Chase began the Crime-Solving Cousins Mystery series. Sophie and Jessica dodged bad guys as they solved a mystery about a briefcase filled with feathers.

Shannon enjoys hiking and shopping, and both chocolate and fruit, so parts of her personality are in Sophie and Jessica. She lives in Nashville, Tennessee, with her professor husband and adorable calico cat.

CPSIA information can be obtained
at www.ICGtesting.com
Printed in the USA
BVOW08s2325041117
499563BV00001B/6/P